VANILLA

VANILLA EXTRACT

VANILLA EXTRACT

Louisa Berry

VANILLA EXTRACT

Text Copyright © Louisa Berry 2017

Louisa Berry has asserted her right in accordance with the Copyright Designs and Patents Act 1988 to be identified as the author of this work.

All rights reserved

No part of this publication may be lent, resold, hired out or reproduced in any form or by any means without prior written permission from the author and publisher. All rights reserved.
Copyright © 3P Publishing

First published in 2017 in the UK

3P Publishing
C E C, London Road
Corby
NN17 5EU

A catalogue number for this book is available from the British Library

ISBN 978-1-911559-30-6

Cover design: Jamie Rae

Cover photography by Alan R Horten

VANILLA EXTRACT

To the bravest woman I ever met (my mother, Jacqueline) whose wings were clipped way too early.

VANILLA EXTRACT

VANILLA EXTRACT

Contents:

Acknowledgements
Prologue
Chapter 1 - Latex Man   1
Chapter 2 - Snake Hips   33
Chapter 3 - Tim Sexy Policeman   44
Chapter 4 - Tattooed Temptation   56
Chapter 5 - Chicken Dinner   77
Chapter 6 - Impale Me!   84
Chapter 7 - Girl Friends   100
Chapter 8 - Close Call   110
Chapter 9 - Pearls of Wisdom   119
Chapter 10 - Brandon, Anthony and Lou   140
Chapter 11 - School Disco!   154
Chapter 12 - False Marketing   168
Chapter 13 - Pablo   172
Chapter 14 - Mr Fit   183
Chapter 15 - Underground Encounter   191
Chapter 16 - Italian Adventures   196
Chapter 17 - Rules of Disengagement   225

VANILLA EXTRACT

Acknowledgments:

Where to begin exactly? Firstly I would like to thank the friends who have stuck with me and listened to my stories before they ever made it into print. To those whose ears I chewed off during and following the research I undertook, particularly Mandy, Alexandra, Luciana, Louise and Shantell. They managed to stay interested whilst I recounted my discoveries and their reactions reiterated the need to document my findings. They also kept me grounded and sane (ish) in the debaucherous world I entered.

Thank you to Elaine, who again listened, and encouraged me to carry on writing. She gave me the confidence to continue after she read the earliest of words - laughing in Pizza Express and Costa during my lunch breaks. She said the previously-considered 'seedy' topic was now humanised, relatable and at times funny. Humour really can be found in some weird and wonderful places (although not all places in this book are bathed in light or fairy dust).

Next is Muna, who I thank for providing the first male response to my words, as well as keeping me on my toes to realising my goal and completing the book. (Not that I wouldn't have finished it without him.) It was interesting to hear a male perspective on what was scribed. Women - I'm just hoping I haven't given away too many of our secrets!

Alan, I thank for his beautiful photography and attention to detail. His wit never ceases to amuse

VANILLA EXTRACT

me and his wise counsel is always valued.

My appreciation goes to those who permitted me to recount their tales. I hope our readers find them as entertaining as we did. (Names have been changed where requested.)

A huge Thank You to the 'Flavas' and the 'Unicorns', for the fun times and banter – long may they continue.

To my family, I am eternally grateful for your love, laughter, friendship and sheer craziness. Please never change. You fill my life with discovery and laughter, and I love you all to bits.

*And thank **you** for giving this book your time and attention. I hope you enjoy the adventures and misadventures you discover before you.*

Louisa Berry

VANILLA EXTRACT

Prologue

This could really be it. Snuggled up on his sofa on a cold Sunday afternoon watching a film. It felt so natural, so right. The log fire raging, red wine flowing, she was completely at ease in his arms. She knew he was a good man. She could tell, even though it was only weeks into this new relationship. He was honest, reliable and kind and he had huge potential as her partner, not to mention a body to die for. So why in the back of her mind did this niggling question keep raising its weary head? Instead of enjoying the moment and melting further into his well-defined chest, over and over again she wondered: "Should I send the black latex catsuit back...?"

It was a reasonable dilemma, she thought. He didn't strike her as the kind of man who would be into that sort of kink, and maybe it was time for her to settle down after all; move away from the life of debauchery she had begun since her marriage broke down a year or so before. But was she ready to give that up? Was it too soon? Could she be 'vanilla' again? There were so many items on her 'list' still to achieve before being sensible, responsible, maybe even rational again – the Matrix catsuit for starters!

VANILLA EXTRACT

Chapter 1: Latex Man

Obviously 'Latex Man' wasn't his real name, but it was the one she came to remember him by. She had first discovered him on the online site she subscribed to. (It wasn't a normal dating site, but a very adult one, used for people to hook up for sex.) They had chatted a few times over the past three months or so.

Described as '36, athletic, professional man seeks fun,' he came across as very articulate whenever they exchanged messages. To add to the intrigue, his gallery left her wanting more. It showed body shots in various poses, all semi-clad or bare-chested, but with none of the obvious 'cock' shots that were two a penny on there. As for the amount of erect penises she had seen on the site, it was refreshing that he didn't display any. Perhaps there were some classy people on this site after all? He had an air of cheeky confidence to his profile, as he declared, 'I won't bite unless you really want me to.' It brought a sparkle to her eye when she read it.

Their conversations online had gone from inquisitive chat to mild flirtation, progressing to the more devious acts they would like to carry out with each other. She felt there was more to him than some of the other 'cubs' she was chatting to, who

VANILLA EXTRACT

often told her how they would show her a good time, with their youthful bodies and increased stamina. But Latex Man, despite his younger years, seemed far more mature and there was obviously a connection, as she had taken the extra step and given him her telephone number. This was something she very rarely did as she prided herself on her security and the last thing she needed was hassle from some young wannabe stalker!

They took their conversations away from the site and sent the odd message on Whatsapp, and exchanged a few of the more risque photographs. A few attempts to meet had fallen through for whatever reason, mainly due to them both holding down full-time City jobs and the usual demands of their respective busy lives. What also made it difficult was that the site had so much on offer! She was handed other avenues to pursue very readily. As a single female on there, she was soon distracted by the numerous approaches she had on a daily basis, and Latex Man became less of a priority to her.

She was flicking through her 'friends' one Thursday evening after work. The house was empty, and her addictive nature led her straight back to the site. It was easy to get sucked in and now was no exception. Her inbox was full of praise from complete strangers, and soon she was striking up conversations that could go whichever way she wanted them to. That was the benefit (and sometimes a complete pain in the arse) of being outnumbered by men online. The

VANILLA EXTRACT

site provided an ego boost on demand and tonight that was just what she wanted.

Latex Man was online. Whilst she hadn't spoken to him for a while, she was once again drawn to his profile photograph. It showed a full-length back view, completely naked, carrying an empty coffee jug back to what she presumed was his kitchen. She had seen this picture a number of times before, but on this particular occasion, she found herself transfixed. The innocence of such a routine act was suddenly unusually sexy, and she couldn't take her eyes off him. In a moment of acute spontaneity, she decided to send him a message saying exactly that. "I love that pic. It's so sexy! That's all! Have a great evening." As it disappeared in the ethers, she had a huge and very childish grin on her face. She had no intention of having a conversation at that point; she had run before the 'perving' of the evening had begun. She was just giving complimentary credit where it was due and boy it looked like it was due here. His lean physique and pert bottom looked incredibly appealing. It was rude not to send him the praise!

Lying there in the bubbles she wondered whether it was usual behaviour to take your iPad into the bathroom? Did other people do this? Or was her addiction and need for attention so strong that she couldn't wait until she got out? Either way, she was pleased she had, because before not too long, she noticed her inbox had a number of new messages,

VANILLA EXTRACT

and the one that excited her most was from Latex Man.

"Hello beautiful and thanks. I always make coffee in the nude you know. You should try it some time. I'll make it just how you like it," he greeted her with. She had no doubt in her mind that he would too. It brought an instant smile to her face and a slight tingle in her loins. Why had she lost contact with him? He was fun and definitely worth looking into further. She had forgotten his wit and how he had amused her a few times online, and their earlier saucier conversations about exploring each other's bodies.

Drying her hands, she replied, "White, no sugar. Are you providing the cream?" It was too obvious and too easy, but she couldn't resist. "I can give you more than that on Saturday afternoon if you are free," came his response. Whoosh – a wave of excitement swept over her. She had no plans for Saturday and toyed with the idea of meeting him. Immediately after the instant glee, she suddenly felt nervous and wondered what the hell she was doing? In equally rapid time, her spontaneous nature kicked in, and she said, "I look forward to meeting you on Saturday then." And there it was - round two of more nervous eagerness setting in. "Fantastic. Let me message you the finer details tomorrow, but I can't wait to finally meet you and spend some quality time licking every inch of your body. And if you have any plans for Saturday evening, you might want to cancel them. You might just want to rest

VANILLA EXTRACT

instead ha ha!" What a tease he was, but it was having the right effect. Her mind was now racing, wondering what on earth he had planned and, equally, what was she doing agreeing to this?

She went to bed that night with a cheeky smile on her face because she felt so incredibly naughty. This wasn't the way her friends behaved on a school night! It felt different. It was giving her a buzz, and she couldn't help feeling just a little bit pleased with herself. She had managed to come across as confident and knowing exactly what she wanted, which was actually almost true – apart from the odd moment of doubt! She knew that she didn't want the trappings of a relationship. She just wanted fun, and this seemed to be giving her options to indulge in exactly what she desired, whether it was with younger men, women, various cultures and races, gym fit bodies, whatever. She felt like a small child in a sweet shop, looking up at all the different varieties and not knowing which to pick. So many lovely choices and she was just barely making her first. How many more would she choose in time, she wondered? She guessed that decision would be made following her Saturday encounter.

Friday was a bit of a blur. At the same time, it seemed to drag and while she managed to make her way through her office work, she couldn't get him out of her mind. Latex Man messaged her in the evening, and the arrangements for Saturday were confirmed. They would meet at 1pm at Victoria Station at the top of the Underground station exit.

VANILLA EXTRACT

He would be waiting for her and would show her to his hotel, providing there was the right chemistry between them first of all. This made her feel less uneasy. Meeting in a public place was her first rule. This gave her the option to leave and go about her business if she just didn't fancy him, when they met in the flesh, as it were. The same applied to him of course. This meet gave no guarantees of any sexual activity to follow.

Saturday morning was difficult, not in getting out of bed, but trying to co-ordinate the usually quite simple activities. The anticipation and nerves were playing tricks on a normally straightforward routine. She rose early, too early in fact. She certainly didn't need to wake at 7am on her day off, but in reality, this was still a lay-in compared with her usual weekday alarm call. Muesli it was as she ran a bath. She didn't want to feel too bloated but knew she had to eat something. After taking a few mouthfuls, she had to leave it. She just couldn't face it right now, not with her stomach doing somersaults.

Some maintenance down below was next in the form of a trim before the bath. He had mentioned that he preferred some pubic hair to 'bald pussies', so she now found herself quite relieved when her pre-meet waxing appointment was cancelled the day before. It may have been too late anyway. A wax that soon to a meet could have been risky. She wouldn't have wanted to look swollen for him, and sometimes a wax could do just that, as the sensitive skin cried out for pain relief!

VANILLA EXTRACT

Legs and armpits were next. She headed to the bath and lost the stubble she had started cultivating two days before. Duly covered in a generous layer of body butter, she put on her white cotton dressing gown and made a nice cup of tea. Surely this would settle her nerves? She tried again with the remaining muesli, but it wasn't happening. It seemed her tummy wasn't sure about today either. Even her bladder was confused. Surely she didn't need to go again (and again). It wasn't like the numerous loo visits were exactly productive! One more for the road, and one more it seemed before she eventually got out of the front door!

A few messages were exchanged in the morning, which was helpful. She did not have a clue what to wear! He told her to come in whatever was comfortable, remembering that it was a Saturday afternoon in busy London. He wasn't expecting stockings and suspenders, well not on this occasion at least. Phew! That was a relief, she thought, but she still wanted to wear heels. They accentuated the great curves of her legs, so she went for black suede open cut sandals with a 4" heel. Casual, smart and just the right height, they had been tried and tested for work a number of times. She knew they were very comfortable and wouldn't give her any grief as she negotiated the tube, escalators, stairs and uneven pavements. Accompanied by a tight-fitting pair of jeans, was her smart baggy shirt. Fortunately, her toenails were still clinging onto that dark blue varnish she had painted them with earlier in the week. Her fingernails required a little bit of

VANILLA EXTRACT

touching up, and she had plenty of time to make them look beautiful. She wondered if he'd even notice, but she preferred to have them immaculate rather than her being conscious of them later.

The anticipation was rising. Her hands were clammy; she forgot where she put her keys, and even her handbag too had decided to have a quick game of hide and seek. But it was fine. She had plenty of time still, despite all of these niggles she could do without. Even a phone call from her brother had to be cut short as she had too much on her mind and so much to do still, including straightening her hair, and finally apply the bare minimum of makeup, i.e. mascara. It was a Saturday afternoon – she wasn't exactly getting dolled up for an event. By the end of their meeting she half expected to have her usually wavy hair again and no makeup whatsoever.

Half an hour passed quickly as she drove a fair way to the London suburbs to Redbridge Underground Station. Parking there was to make her life easier. It meant she was a little closer and could get straight onto the Tube network rather than parking at an overground station nearer to where she lived. Getting home would be less hassle later too, at whatever time that was.

Singing her heart out in the car did nothing to dispel the nerves that continued to grow, but it did make the journey disappear rapidly. It was a similar story when she sat on the Tube. The stops were passing quickly, and before she knew it, she had arrived at

VANILLA EXTRACT

Victoria station. She took a deep breath. This really was happening!

Filled to the brim with both anxiety and excitement, the adrenalin bubbling up inside her had started to rise as she rode the escalator to daylight. The other half of her couldn't quite believe she was going through with this. What if there was no sexual chemistry between them? What if he looked nothing like his other pictures? He may not find her attractive in person. What if she was too old for him? He was nine years younger, which had given her an ego boost at the time when she found out, but what if the gap was too much? Either way, it was too late now. She had committed to meet him, and she was not in the habit of letting people down.

Latex Man was on time, as she knew he would be. Amid the hustle and bustle of one of London's busiest train stations, she picked him out almost instantly. Dressed in tight black jeans and a smart black shirt, he looked very chic and oozed sex appeal. He was walking towards her as she made her way up the stairs and finally out of the station. Confidence emanating with each stride he said, "You must be Lou, I take it," as he put his hands on her shoulders, drew her close to him and kissed both cheeks. "I'm so glad you made it. You look absolutely lovely."

Feeling as light as a feather, Lou tried to play it cool. She didn't want to make it too obvious how she felt or show herself up. At moments like this, she was

VANILLA EXTRACT

likely to trip or drop something and give away the calm, confident air she was trying to pull off here. "Thank you," she said graciously.

The usual chaos of the hectic train station continued around them. People busy getting on with their lives, with important engagements and places to go. Natives and tourists checking train platforms, purchasing tickets, visiting the shops and some looking bewildered and lost. It tickled and delighted her to know that not one single passer-by would ever guess that these two strangers were meeting for the first time and under such illicit circumstances. This just added to her excitement, although she didn't know quite what to do with it.

The conversation began as he led her out of the station, linking arms with her as they walked out onto the street. Lou felt instantly comfortable and was very happy to adopt this 'couple look' as they ambled off. It added to the disguise she felt she was now wearing for those at the crowded station. He explained that he was in London for a wedding reception that evening and had a very swanky hotel room booked just around the corner. Perfect!

As they walked in the direction of the hotel, he suggested going for a drink first. Brilliant idea, she thought, as a cool glass of Sauvignon Blanc would help settle the butterflies in her stomach. It was a lovely day too, and it wasn't like she had to get back for her children, so why not? He led her to a very typical old English style pub, the name of which she

VANILLA EXTRACT

would soon forget after this adventure. They went inside, and he asked her what she cared to drink. Now came the awkward moment. Did she offer to go Dutch or just accept his chivalry? "Thanks. I'll get the next one then," she commented after placing her order. "No worries," he said as he asked for a pint of Guinness to go with her wine.

Glasses in hands, they made their way to the seated area outside. The sun was shining and it felt warm on the skin. For a summer's day in England, it was actually rather pleasant, which is something you can't guarantee!

He told her he thought she was incredibly attractive and how pleased he was that she agreed to meet with him after all this time. He was sick of all the time-wasters that he had encountered on the site. In the spirit of embracing compliments instead of making excuses for them, Lou thanked him. She had been taught many moons ago on a Women's Development course that you should show gratitude for kind words, instead of being embarrassed by them or brushing them off. Too often women would rather make excuses than simply say, "Thank you."

They spoke of a similar, allegedly more up-market online site that was set up for the 'sexual elite'. It was one where you had to apply to join, with membership being granted only if you were approved. He told her that she would easily become a member, given her beautiful face and great body

VANILLA EXTRACT

and Lou was flattered. He suggested she go online and apply; it would be easy and free. Men had to pay a membership fee. All very unfair it seemed, but it meant the men would be serious and of a certain calibre, higher than on their current site. This was something Lou had been thinking about for a while and may explore later when she returned home, should she feel the urge (or remote memory or inclination of it, as events transpired).

He also mentioned his love of latex and how she would look good in it. It was a type of clothing she had never had the pleasure of experiencing before, but now she was intrigued. He told her about parties that were held where every attendee would be adorned in this texture and how exciting it was not to know what people looked like underneath their latex masks. This was opening up a whole new world to her, which she knew absolutely nothing about. When he showed her some pictures on his phone of him fully kitted out in the garments, his nickname of Latex Man was born.

Well, this was going rather swimmingly, Lou thought. He was intelligent, funny and had a great personality. While he wasn't the usual gym-fit, muscly type she had been talking with, he was very lean, and she could see his arms were strong. His dark hair contrasted with his tanned skin and his green eyes looked enticing in the sunshine. Wearing all black made him look part Italian or Portuguese. She wondered what combination of different cultures had produced this gorgeous looking man or

VANILLA EXTRACT

was she just getting carried away here with her adventure? He was probably born and bred in London, as were generations of his family before him. Either way, to her he looked hot, hot, hot and she was so pleased she'd had the balls to come out today.

It was now her turn to go get the drinks in. Lou was relieved to have her black jeans on now, as she straddled her way back up from the barbeque style bench and table. That would have been interesting in a skirt and very unlikely that she would have maintained any lady-like decorum when getting up and down from the table! Drink number two was going down easier than the first, and the conversation was certainly flowing too.

When he returned from the toilet, he did something that would remain in her memory (and between her legs) for the rest of her life. Instead of continuing their very natural dialogue, still standing, he reached down to where she was sitting and put his hand around the back of her head, beneath the nape of her neck. Pulling her face towards him, he lent down and gave her the most passionate kiss she had ever experienced in her 44 years. His tongue delved deep inside her mouth, and she instantly melted. It was like a wave of intensity washing over her entire body. Lou reciprocated, plunging her tongue inside his mouth. It felt amazing to find someone who would offer up his mouth completely - not just partially open for a quick tongue fight. Instead, this kiss was fiery, delicious and left her tingling from

VANILLA EXTRACT

head to toe as he slowly withdrew. "Wow," escaped her mouth before she could hold it back in. "That was pure passion," she said, and he smiled at her, knowing exactly what she meant.

He sat down opposite her once more and continued talking, but the contract had just been sealed tight. There was now an inner buzzing running through her, and she was finding it hard to control. Her foot kept tapping under the table like it was caught on a nerve. There was now a knowing between them that they definitely had a sexual chemistry and were about to embark on something tantalizing.

Urgency now came to their encounter. The calm small talk and getting to know each other was replaced by the most basic of instincts. Carnal desire began to pump through her veins, and it needed to be addressed now!

The rest of their drinks were gulped down, and he gave her directions to his hotel. It would be better if he arrived there first and she came up to his room. Lou did not question this but instead was happy to follow his lead. Eccleston Square was only a few minutes walk, and she would be there in no time. His instructions were for Lou to leave in fifteen minutes, which of course she obeyed. Kissing her gently on her cheek, he stood up and walked away.

Lou was not sure if it was the speed at which she had drunk two glasses of wine, the sun beating down on her face, or the hunger she felt for him, but her

VANILLA EXTRACT

cheeks were glowing bright red! Sitting there trying to calm herself down, she couldn't help but smile at what had just happened. There was also some activity in her knickers. She knew he had stirred her and her body was naturally preparing for him. Hot and sticky, her underwear would surely give her away when they came to it! Lou felt vibrant, and she also felt alive. There was no better feeling than this right now!

Fifteen minutes can take an awfully long time when you are in this state of excitement. Lou refrained from looking at her watch each and every one of those long, drawn-out minutes. Instead, she alternated between phone and watch, checking the time but also to see if he had left any message. Ten rather painfully slow minutes later and her phone pinged. It was Latex Man. "I'm ready for you now. Leave the pub and come to my room. It's 201, and you can come straight up the stairs. No need to look or talk to reception. Just head straight up."

Struggling to contain her eagerness, she shot up and left the pub. The nerves and/or the drink were kicking in as she walked to his hotel. Unfortunately, she completely missed the entrance and found herself completing an entire circuit of the square, only to arrive back where she started. What a fool! Fortunately, second time round, she noticed the hotel sign and casually walked in and up the stairs as he had instructed. Lou was a little sweatier than she had hoped, but it was too late to do anything about that now. She could always put it down to being so turned on!

Room 201 overlooked the square, and she wondered if he had seen her walk straight past. How embarrassing would that be? He'd have thought she had lost the plot, or lost the bottle and was too afraid to come in.

He opened the door to her and she felt more at ease. He looked and smelt terrific. She decided to come clean and told him about her mini adventure there in the square. She put it down to being a little flustered, and he told her it was totally natural and nothing to worry about. He was kind too - what a relief!

Before she could say anymore, he swept her into the room and forced her up against the wall. His tongue was deep inside her mouth and hands placed either side of her jaw. The adrenalin inside her was about to explode. Kissing him fervently back, she dropped her bag onto the floor, with a loud thud. Right now, it really didn't matter what had just landed awkwardly in there.

Pulling her top over her head and off, he began to passionately kiss her neck and then down to her chest. Her nipples were erect as he reached into her bra and fondled her breast, as he continued to kiss her tenderly. Lou could not help but flinch. Her whole body was consumed with desire. Leaning down he gently nibbled the nipple, sending currents

VANILLA EXTRACT

straight to her clitoris. Her body reverberated once more. Back to her mouth, his tongue seeking hers, he pulled her arms above her head, pushed them back and continued delving deep. This was mind-blowing. They were both horny as hell.

Unlike the movies, getting her skin-tight trousers off didn't quite go according to plan. He unbuttoned them and pulled them down to reveal her black Brazilian panties. The lace looked amazing on her peach-like bum, and she wondered if he realised he licked his lips in approval. Peeling the jeans off proved more difficult, particularly as he wanted her to keep her heels on. Now was not the time for her jeans to act like they were stuck with super glue. To facilitate, she slipped the shoes off, stripped off the jeans and threw them onto the floor. "Let's pretend that didn't happen," Lou joked as she put the shoes back on and returned to her position at the wall.

He had taken the opportunity to remove his shirt and was looking very masculine with his chest exposed. It was getting far too hot in here to leave any shred of clothing on. His arms were toned and strong, and she looked forward to them being around her, even with the veins protruding somewhat in all this drama. His trousers were next to come off - fortunately much easier to remove than hers had been. Lou could see his rather huge penis poking out of the top of his Hugo Boss pants, proving that Latex Man was just as turned on as she was. Delicately slipping her fingers in each side of his pants, she dropped to her knees and guided

VANILLA EXTRACT

them over his manhood as she pulled them down. Out he slipped, and she fully anticipated going down on him there and then. She was keen to see how he tasted. "Not yet," he said as he reached down to her waist and drew her back up to standing. "I'm not done with you," he said, as he placed her hands back above her head and continued kissing.

His tongue was like velvet; so smooth and silky in her mouth. Slowly and passionately he licked his way down to her throat and onto her breasts once more. This time he unbuttoned Lou's bra, and her hands lowered to allow it to drop to the floor. She raised her arms back up again herself, although he was not restraining her now. Taking her right breast in his hand, he noticed the piercing of the left. He nodded in approval as his tongue began to caress the bar, licking and flicking slowly; sending shivers straight through her to her more delicate areas. Sweeping across, he squeezed both her breasts as he came back up to her face to continue his feast.

His hand went into her knickers as he kissed her. Lou was a trembling wreck, and lowering her arms, she placed them on the back of his head and pulled him in tight to kiss deeper, if this was even possible. His fingertips began tickling her clitoris, and she gasped with delight. It was completely uncontrollable and rather louder than she anticipated, but it just came out! She wondered if he would approve and his smile indicated that he absolutely did.

VANILLA EXTRACT

A rhythm was building with his fingers on her, and before she knew it, she was rotating her hips. "Someone's getting excited," he said as he plunged a digit deep inside her. Another involuntary intake of air escaped her, as she squealed with pleasure and began to grind her pelvis onto his hand. Still kissing her, he withdrew from her now sodden panties and sucked his guilty finger. "You taste like honey," he said as he put it in her mouth, followed once more by his tongue. He was right. She did taste sweet. She had tasted it before over the years, but this was possibly the most erotic time ever.

Dropping to his knees, he pulled her panties to one side. "Now I want to really taste you." Before she could comment, Lou felt the tingling again down there on her 'bean.' Flicking his tongue from side to side, she was getting more and more aroused. The intensity was rising, and she was finding it difficult to balance against the wall as her body flinched even more sporadically and with much more force.

Boom! There he was. Tongue now deep inside her, lapping up her juices. Oh boy, this was amazing and naughty too – leaving her knickers on and quite happily drenching them through! Slipping two fingers inside her, he returned to licking her most sensitive part and began to build up the rotation once more.

Lou wondered if he might make her cum there and then. That would be a first. Normally it took bloody ages for her body to finally let go and for the

VANILLA EXTRACT

trumpets' fanfare and the sparkling confetti to fall from the skies. Men really did have to put in the legwork for that treat, which did get a bit frustrating for her too at times. Invariably her right hand would wander down to assist when required to get her over the final hurdle. Today might just be different, she hoped.

"I want you laying down," he said and picked her up. He was as strong as she suspected. Her immediate reaction was to wrap her legs around him, as he carried her towards the king-size bed where he threw her down upon it. From the bedside cabinet, he took out a blindfold. It was in his preferred colour; black and was made of silk. "I want you to wear this," he said as he straddled her and tied it around her eyes. His erect penis brushed across her stomach and groin as he tied it. Lou tried to keep her cool as this sent another tingle straight through her. The blindfold felt soft and delicate, but she could not see a thing through it. Lou lay down on the pillow and was in a state of excited anticipation. What did he have in store for her now?

Carefully he removed her soaked underwear. Lou wondered if she should be embarrassed by the wilted, wet artefact he placed on the side cabinet? She wasn't, and if she had been, her eyes were covered and would not reveal this secret thought.

Caressing her face tenderly with his lips, he slowly made his way to her neck, where he nibbled and kissed before moving on to her breasts. They were

VANILLA EXTRACT

ripe and ready as before, and he treated them fairly, taking time on one and then the other. Licking her torso, he moved south once more and slowly made his way to the prize. Lou was a sodden mass of desire and wanting. Her body was craving for him to put his cock inside her now, but she knew he wasn't finished with teasing her yet.

Grabbing the Victorian headboard, she held on tight. This was getting intense. His attention was on her clit again, with two fingers inside her, he was building her up once more for that crescendo. Flicking, nibbling and sucking, her body was resisting the urge to explode there and then. Deeper inside the fingers probed, and her grinding took on a new level. She was absorbed in the moment, and she knew she was getting close. Surely the point of letting go completely would be upon her soon?

Wrapping her hands around the back of his head, she pulled him into her vagina, not that he needed to get any deeper. Hanging on for dear life, his rhythm gained momentum. Fingers penetrating, tongue lapping, she was almost there. If only she could just free this euphoria? Biting her lip, she relaxed into the motion, when another wave of intensity flooded her body. Oh yes, it was so close. As this thought went through her mind, her body concurred, and whoa, here it came. "Oh yes, yes, I'm cumming," she shrieked as her body tensed up and released an almighty orgasm. His lapping increased as he held her down, despite her uncontrollable wriggling. This was a powerful

VANILLA EXTRACT

explosion. It wasn't relenting yet and as he continued to drink her juice. Her body was keen to quench his thirst.

Her legs began to shake violently in shock as he continued to maintain his licking. Fighting, she could take no more. This was too much. What broke the spell were her giggles. Lou could not help it. They just came naturally. This was obviously a huge release for her, not just sexually but emotionally too. What an amazing stress-relief!

As the intensity began to subside, she removed the blindfold and joked, "Oh it's you." Happily laughing she felt totally exposed now, but it was of no concern. She felt fantastic! Looking down and seeing him for the first time in a while, Lou was pleased to see that he was smiling too, with a face that was completely saturated! Wiping away her juices from his cheeks and chin, he slid up her body and gave her another deep kiss. Again she could taste herself on him. In fact, it was all around her mouth now too as well as inside it. Just as well she didn't mind. Her body was now calming down, though still trembling in the aftermath.

"Your turn," Lou said, as she gestured for him to lay down now and command the position at the centre of the bed. Still buzzing from her own explosion, she wanted him to feel as special as she did. Fully intending to take as long as possible, she straddled his waist. The temptation was to go straight to his genitalia, but she had plenty of time for that. Right

VANILLA EXTRACT

now her focus was on making her way to his mouth. Sliding up his chest, she brushed her breasts against him as she began to lick his nipples. Erect and sensitive, she kissed them delicately, and then continued to lick up to his neck and then onto his lips. She resisted the urge to force her tongue straight inside, instead licked around his lip area, circling ever so gently. She could feel his erect penis throbbing beneath her. He wanted her attention.

His mouth was ready for her as she charged her tongue between his lips. Hands now either side of his head, Lou held him steady as she began to explore inside. His body began to move, hips grinding below her. This was dangerous ground as it would be all too easy to climb aboard and let him deep inside her. But both of them valued their safety and had already had the discussion online about practicing safe sex.

Instead, she withdrew from his mouth and began to work her way down his athletic body. His neck was first, gentle caressing with her lips, down to his chest once more. Never leaving out the nipples, they received some more focus before she dragged her tongue along the surface of his skin down past the obvious place and to his inner left thigh. Hair sweeping over him, tickling him with its gentle touch, Lou began to bite his skin softly. It wasn't rough or painful but sent shivers through him. He let out a gentle moan, as he pushed his groin area up into the air. Licking up to his stomach, she again swept over him to the right thigh and began again.

VANILLA EXTRACT

His cock was feeling neglected and ready as it pointed to the ceiling waiting for her tongue. Instead, her cheek brushed against him. Looking up and smiling, he noticed how she was enjoying teasing him so.

Now it was time for her tongue to work its magic on him. His cock was dribbling now in anticipation. Clear sticky pre-cum was escaping from the tip of his shaft as she slowly began licking this off and carrying on down to his balls and back up again. She ran her hands up his stomach and tweaked his nipples. She could tell he wanted to be inside her mouth now, but she wasn't ready to give him that pleasure. Taking her time up and down, she moved back across his groin and forced her tongue inside his belly button. He gasped, sighed and then laughed as it has made him cringe ever so slightly. Lou smiled too and then went back to her prize.

Hungrily taking his cock in her mouth, she grabbed his balls and massaged them in time with her hard sucking. His entire body curled up as his back arched with delight. "Fuck me!" he shouted out as his back returned to the bed. "Oh I intend to," she replied and then continued, but eased off on the pressure. Gently licking up and down his penis again, she took the head into her mouth and grabbed his penis in her left hand. Holding it tightly, she pressed down hard with her tongue and felt him shudder beneath her. To-ing and fro-ing, she licked down on the tip before releasing her grip and then sucking slowly up and down. He moaned

VANILLA EXTRACT

with pleasure as she began to build up momentum. Faster and deeper she moved on him. His hand came down on the back of her head now, pushing himself deeper into her mouth as she gagged. It had brought tears to her eyes, and she knew it would likely have made her mascara run ever so slightly. Withdrawing, she used the extra saliva to lubricate him as she slid her right hand up and down him. He was bulging and ready to pop!

Wondering whether she should go down and spend more time giving oral to the ball area and beyond, Lou decided to keep that pleasure to herself. She didn't want to go giving out all her best skills on the first encounter, although she had a feeling he would enjoy rimming and more. This was something she would keep up her sleeve for now.

"I think you should get on top," he said, and she absolutely agreed. Reaching over to the bedside cabinet, he produced a condom, which he started to open aggressively. Once in place, Lou crouched above him and slowly lowered herself onto his throbbing cock, careful to maintain eye contact as he entered her. This was intense. His cock felt huge inside her; ever more sensitive as it went further in. Slowly she began to lower and raise herself onto him, gasping as it reached the top. "Ooh that feels so good," she said quietly, almost a whisper as she started to build up some pace.

While it did feel fantastic for both of them, Lou knew she couldn't maintain this crouched position for too long before her thighs started to ache. She brought her knees to the bed and continued to ride, straddled across him. It felt even deeper like this, and she was surprised to find that she appeared to be leaking clear fluid onto his stomach. Unsure what exactly it was, she was relieved that he seemed completely at ease with it. "I don't mind if you want to gush on me," he said and whilst it felt a little strange to be blatantly saturating him, she was happy to carry on, no matter how soaked the bed sheet beneath them was becoming. It wasn't like she would be sleeping here tonight – so not really her concern!

Lou was dripping perspiration as well, as she was riding him on top. The motion and the rubbing were affecting her clit once more. In fact, she felt positively tingly again and wondered if she would cum in this position. Years ago she had achieved it, but it was rare. As she was persevering, digging deeper into him as she rocked back and forth, she began to feel light-headed. Maybe it was the temperature in the humid hotel room, or maybe it was the excitement and cardio workout she was having. Either way, she was drenched and needed to calm it down a little. With him still inside her, she drew herself slowly down, and she slid her breasts up from his stomach and along to his sweaty chest. Back up to his mouth, she kissed him forcefully; tongues colliding with passion as they were now skin on skin and entwined most intimately.

VANILLA EXTRACT

Lou was right about his solid arms. He soon managed to pick her up, whip her around and lay her on her back sideways on the bed. With his feet firmly on the ground, he grabbed her hips, pulled them back to the edge of the bed and lined her up for him. Next, without any conversation or hesitation, he rammed his stiff cock inside her. He was back in control and was relishing this moment.

Crying out in delight, she sunk her nails into his buttocks and drew him into her. He bit his lip and stared at her intently. Sheer determination showed on his face as he began to pound her harder and harder. "Wow, that's deep," Lou almost whimpered as she felt him reach the top of her cervix. Gripping onto the bed sheets, they provided no support, but they did give her hands something to hold on to as he thrust fully inside.

She was gasping harder now as he continued to slam into her. Putting his hands underneath her, he lifted up her hips now, so his penis probed even further inside. Shrieking with delight, she went along with this new forceful motion, as he began his own workout, pulling her body onto him with every thrust. He certainly had the stamina, and she smiled to herself. It was obvious why she went for the younger man these days!

Eager to have her every way he could, he spun her over. Lou was keen to please and raised her bottom up in the air, so she was on all fours. He now had easy access, but before he entered her, he gave her a bit of a surprise. Instead of slipping his cock inside straight away, he lowered his face into her groin area and licked her clit once more. Electricity passed through her immediately, with a force so strong that her body shuddered at the touch of his tongue and almost knocked him off her. He laughed at first, and then repeated the naughty tasting, this time slipping at least one finger inside her vagina. It was hard for her to tell exactly how many.

Withdrawing however many digits it was, Lou didn't have to wait long before he filled her up with much more. Even deeper inside, she could feel his natural weapon battering her innards, and it felt wonderful. He reached down and grabbed her hair. Pulling it gently at first, she felt slightly out of control, but it was good. As the speed increased, so did the force of hair tugging. Somewhat uncomfortable, it was also turning her on, being slightly restricted, and receiving his full power. He was enjoying the thrill, as the intensity increased and the sweat began rolling down his face and dripping onto her back.

He was close now. Dropping her hair, he grabbed her hips tighter and again pulled her into him. Crashing himself into her, he maintained the momentum until he was ready to unload. "Oh, oh, I'm gonna cum Lou," he declared as he gave a final thrust to victory! Almost in slow motion now compared with the chaos of before, there was a moment of pause, as he tensed inside her. Next, the shuddering began as he hit release. Lou could feel

VANILLA EXTRACT

his body ricochet from way within as he held her body tight. Now they were one.

When the aftershocks subsided, he withdrew himself slowly, removed the condom and placed it on the side. He would sort that out after. Right now he just wanted to be horizontal again, and she was keen to oblige him, shifting on the bed to the being-spooned position. He wrapped his arms around her, and they laid there entwined for a while before either had the energy or inclination to continue with any form of conversation.

At moments like this Lou presumed most women would want cuddles and affection. Her friends often shared their joy at those post-coital moments when they felt dreamy and at one with their partner. That was how it used to be when she made love with her husband. However, more recently she had been told on a number of occasions that she thought like a man, which she saw as a bonus. What they (usually men) meant by this was that she was able to divorce herself from the emotional ties of intercourse. Sex in her eyes was literally just that - sex. It was fun. It was passionate. It was incredibly messy, and she knew exactly what it wasn't under circumstances like these, and that was 'love'. This did not mean she enjoyed it any less. In fact, she thrived on it, but she was under no illusion either.

So after a while of feeling completely relaxed, she said, "Well that was pretty fucking amazing. Thank you".

VANILLA EXTRACT

"No need to thank me. I completely agree,' he affirmed, and she was very pleased to hear it. With arms and legs wrapped around each other, she enjoyed the feeling of safety and contentment. Lou didn't particularly want to move, and she wondered if she could just stay here for the rest of the day, but she knew she would have to get going soon. He was stroking her shoulder gently now. He was being very tender, and it was a shame that she did have to go, but then she reminded herself that you could never have too much of a good thing. Or could you? She had a feeling that they would have had at least one more round of naughtiness if he didn't have somewhere else to be later.

To ensure no awkward feelings followed, she volunteered, "Best that I jump in the shower then, if you have to get ready." She lifted his arm off of her and untangled their legs. "Afraid so babe. I would have loved if you could have stayed for longer, but I really should be getting my shit together for this wedding." She already anticipated this was coming, so she rolled herself off the bed and made her way to the bathroom.

The shower was beckoning, and she was pleased to oblige. She stood underneath its refreshing and very soothing downpour for some time – longer than she normally would have done at home. Reflecting on the naughty afternoon she had just experienced, she washed away the cocktail of bodily fluids they had shared.

VANILLA EXTRACT

After towel drying, Lou noticed the complimentary body lotion. It smelt fruity and looked expensive, so she liberally applied it all over her skin, including her face, which she was pleased to find did not resemble Alice Cooper following her mascara now being washed (or worn) away. She emerged from the bathroom looking and feeling revitalised.

Casting her eyes around the room, she was able to locate the various items of clothing that had been discarded so eagerly earlier. A slight dilemma faced her as she found her knickers. They were drenched, and she slightly cringed at the thought of putting them back on in that state, but she didn't have much choice other than to go commando. However, given the pounding she had just received, she thought it best not to have her tight jeans chaffing her delicate area! Fortunately, he didn't notice any of this as he headed towards the bathroom himself for a shower.

Gathering the rest of her clothes, she got herself dressed fully and then found the comb in her bag. It was time to tidy up the hair that was still soaking wet and somewhat curlier than when she arrived. She accompanied him in the bathroom and combed it through. "Beautiful," he said, which was the last thing she thought she looked right now, but he was polite at least! She smiled, "Why thank you," she said and moved in to hug him. "I had a great time with you," and kissed him tenderly on the lips. "Well, I hope we can do this again some time when we can spend the whole day and night together," he

VANILLA EXTRACT

replied. He placed one hand either side of her head and kissed her forehead. Oh, she sure hoped so too.

The kettle had been put on when she was showering, but Lou declined his offer of coffee. "Not unless you have your coffee pot with you," she joked. He saw her to the door where they kissed and hugged again. She made her way down the hotel stairs and outside to the fresh air.

It was almost like she floated on air back to Victoria Station, smiling all the way and feeling rather pleased with herself. What an unbelievable, amazing time she had with Latex Man. It was like a fairy tale of naughtiness, and she absolutely loved the way she felt - fulfilled, contented and adventurous all in one. What made it all the more satisfying was knowing that it was her little secret. Lou couldn't help but beam at all those people on the return tube journey. None of them had the slightest inclination of what she had been up to! This thrill gave her a kick all the way home and way beyond.

VANILLA EXTRACT

Chapter Two - Snake Hips

Working in finance, Lou came across many wannabe Gordon Gecko types, sadly not matching up in the quality of the clothing they adorned, or their intellect either. In fact, subconsciously, she had an unwritten rule that she would never date 'suits' as she came to refer to them as. Instead, Lou was more attracted to the more physical profession; roofers, builders, scaffolders and the like. Their manual labour jobs meant they tended to be fitter and more body conscious, which of course she loved in a man. Lou would often find herself walking past a building site and wanting to wolf whistle some of the guys she saw working hard, but that wasn't allowed in this day and age, well not for men to do this to women, but in reverse? She was sure they wouldn't mind! It would no doubt appeal to their egos and humour.

Snake Hips was different. He was immaculately dressed, with an expensive suit that was tailored to fit his carved out body. His crisp shirts hugged his muscular biceps and she could see the shape of his triangular back as he got up from his desk and walked to the printer. His matching tie was fixed with perfection and sat neatly across his broad chest, with what she could only imagine was his six or eight pack below it. She doubted there was any fat

VANILLA EXTRACT

on his body as she visualised him naked. He was sex on legs and she wanted him!

Lou was not sure where he appeared from exactly, suddenly sat in her part of the open plan office where two banks were dedicated for 'hot desking'. It was pot- luck who would appear there every day, and she thought she had certainly won the jackpot when he showed up looking so damned gorgeous. She could smell his aftershave straight away. It was strong, yet refreshing in the work environment. Not many other men she knew would pay that much attention to detail. He was a rare find.

As he pulled his laptop from his man bag and set himself up to log on, Lou stood up and reached across the desk to introduce herself. "Morning, I'm Lou," she said. "I've not seen you here before." He gave his name (but 'Snake Hips' was better, she decided) and explained that he had joined the Close Protection team a few weeks before. They were set up to protect the company's most senior executives and were pretty much all from an ex-military background. That explained a lot, she thought. No wonder he was so well turned out - physically and in the wardrobe department - even his shoes were recently polished, she couldn't help but notice!

A few weeks passed during which she saw him on some of the days she was working in the office when he wasn't busy keeping the elite staff safe. Lou noticed he had that sparkle in his eye when she was around and for some reason, she turned into a giggly

VANILLA EXTRACT

schoolgirl in his presence. 'Keep it together Lou,' she thought, as she remembered that in this style of office layout, her other colleagues could see and hear every comment, flick of the hair and stare across the desk! There was just something about him that she liked and she couldn't help being attracted.

It wasn't long before Lou uttered those immortal and leading words, "We should grab a coffee sometime." She didn't know it then, but this was apparently music to his ears, he later told her. He was itching to get some alone time with her, in whatever capacity, but with this corporate world being so vastly different to that of a combat one, he wasn't sure how to play it. His boss had given some guidance about staying well away from office women, but in his mind, every female in the building was clad in stockings and suspenders, and he was a red-blooded male after all. Regardless of whether this was just, in fact, a figment of his imagination, he still felt a little out of his depth and wasn't sure how to approach trying to get to know Lou better. So when Lou asked him for coffee, he was beaming with happiness – decision made for him!

Canary Wharf, like many other finance hubs, has its fair selection of coffee providers. Rather than draw attention to themselves, Lou arranged to meet him at the smaller of the Costa Coffees near Waitrose. It was a little more intimate than the others in the area and would give them a chance to talk openly, without being overheard or spotted by fellow work

VANILLA EXTRACT

associates.

Snake Hips was in the queue when she arrived. Lou couldn't help but check him out as he stood there. He was rather delicious! She was looking forward to learning more about him. Two skinny lattes onboard and they found a table tucked around the back of the counter. Lou thanked him for the coffee and sat down. He removed his jacket to expose his pristine white fitted shirt with bulging chest beneath and placed it on the back of his chair. Lou had to stop herself from drooling there and then. He oozed sex appeal. 'Composure woman,' she again reminded herself.

And so the conversation flowed... Snake Hips had spent 22 years in the army, serving in Northern Ireland, Falkland Islands, Africa and Afghanistan, to name a few. Having retired from the military, this was his first employment in the business world and he was enjoying keeping the office types safe. It was vastly different, and he was finding the bureaucracy completely alien to him. His career had been spent where action mattered, and decisions were made instantly - very different indeed!

Snake Hips had always kept himself fit and always would. He told her that 'train hard, fight easy' was a motto he continued to live by, not that he hoped for any fighting of the kind he was used to in this new role. The job, like the military, allowed him to train daily and at 39 years old, she thought he looked amazing for his age. Younger men were bound to be

VANILLA EXTRACT

jealous of his physique.

Lou was mesmerised! The more he spoke, the more she hung on to every word. His life experience was completely different to hers and she was fascinated. She was also interested to know about his home life and admitted that she wondered if he was gay. Not to stereotype, but given his spotless attire and dress sense, she had to ask whether the partner he referred to was male or female. Snake Hips laughed when she approached it. "No, I'm straight," he confirmed but admitted they barely did anything in the bedroom department anymore. "My wife's become so used to me working away, that I think she's lost interest. Not only that, but she hasn't got the sex drive to match mine!" 'Now that sounded like a challenge,' Lou thought to herself with a smile.

Lou told him about her life, about her children, their father, her work and her interests. He was shocked to hear the ages of her children and complimented her on getting her figure back. "You've got a great body, Lou," he said and smiled from ear to ear. It was a very cheeky smile and both of them knew what underlying motives were being considered as he spoke – every much by her as well as him.

Following this encounter, technology had a part to play in the proceedings of how they became more than workmates. Internal messaging of the quick-fire variety gave them the mechanism for getting to know each other even further, without those around them listening in. It seemed they had a lot more in

VANILLA EXTRACT

common than they had originally thought as their conversations evolved rapidly and it wasn't long before they both knew they wanted more than just coffee.

The first aid room was the inaugural place for naughtiness. He had familiarised himself with it as part of his work duties, in case he had to administer medical attention. "Meet you there in ten minutes," he messaged her. Instant nervous excitement filled her from head to foot. Lou knew what this meant. They would be crossing the imaginary line of flirting to intimate, however deep a level, and there would be no turning back. What to do? What to do? He was a married man and she knew it, but ultimately he was the one who had to sleep with himself at night – she didn't, and if he was able to live with it, then what difference did it make to her? She already knew the answer. Her conscience was clear. Lou was so horny for him that she was out in the lift area before she knew it and on her way down to the break out floor.

Apprehensively she approached the first aid room. Would he be in there? Would someone else be in there? She could smell his Ralph Lauren Polo, but cautiously she knocked on the door twice - best to check. "Come in," the familiar voice welcomed, as the door opened up before her. Lou walked in cautiously. He locked the door behind her and smiled churlishly at her. "Well, well, well," he said and put his hands either side of her jaw. Pushing her against the door. "I've been waiting to do this

VANILLA EXTRACT

for so long," and forced his tongue inside her mouth. It was deep; it was passionate; it was raw. Lou loved it!

Lou was intoxicated by his pure manliness as well his aftershave. Snake Hips was strong and pure muscle. She breathed in the scenario she found herself in and embraced it completely. Responding immediately, she equally delved her tongue into him; pushing her hips against his. Lou could feel his erection trapped in his suit trousers, as his groin hit hers. Both forcing themselves on each other, it was like the battle of the bulge! He was rock solid she felt as he ground into her. Lou placed her right hand on it. He let out a cool sigh, "Ah, that feels good," and started to unbutton his trousers. She hadn't expected their first encounter to be quite as heated as this, but she was more than happy to continue. She anticipated their initial intimate moment would have just been about kissing, and as fantastic as that was, she knew this was going to be much, much more.

His Under Armour pants inside were a little sticky at the tip of his throbbing penis. She groped him, feeling all the way down his shaft and underneath to his balls. Snake Hips let the elastic loosen as his cock fell out. It was massive, and it was ready. Lou fell to her knees and started to lick his stomach and tops of his thighs. She made her way to his swollen member. His wetness was soon gone as she devoured him whole! Sucking while cupping his scrotum, they were both in their element. "Oh God

VANILLA EXTRACT

that's so good," he said as she began to build up a rhythm. "Don't let me cum yet. I need to feel you first."

Snake Hips pulled away from Lou, as she stood up. It was his turn to kneel. Hitching up her skirt, he revealed her seamed hold-ups. "I knew it," he said. "You just drip sex appeal". She was too lost in the moment to thank him. Now he was slipping her knickers to one side. "There she is. Let me at her." His tongue plunged inside her as he began to lap. 'Oh my God, that's fucking amazing,' she thought. And it did feel so good, but so wrong too – she was at work after all!

Lou had to contain her gasps in case someone outside the room heard. The adrenalin, excitement and passion were all building up together. He was licking faster now to a point she could hold it no more. She didn't want to release it now, but she had no choice. Trying her utmost to stay quiet, she let out a small sigh as she came all over his tongue. It was a hard explosion that made her legs shake as she tried to compose herself when really she wanted to scream out how fantastic it felt!

Given she didn't know him very well, and that they were supposed to be working and could easily be caught, she found herself in a fit of giggles. It was probably because she was a bit embarrassed too, but that really didn't matter now. Lou was buzzing. She felt amazing, albeit very naughty too.

VANILLA EXTRACT

What he did next caught her completely by surprise. Reaching inside her pussy, two fingers up high, he began to vigorously pull his hand to and fro. Lou wasn't exactly sure what he was doing, but it felt pleasant and then it became very intense. It was out of her control and before she knew it, there was clear fluid was running all the way down her left leg. She'd had some experience of this before, but nothing to this degree. It was like a river pouring out of her! "What the fuck is that? Have I just pissed myself? Or is that gush?" Lou was confused. She hadn't felt like she'd emptied her bladder in the slightest, but her left shoe was filling up, and she couldn't explain why. "Yes, it's gush Lou," he said. "I've just made you gush. It's not wee. You're ok. You haven't pissed yourself!" Given she had to go back to her desk, she told him not to do it anymore, though she could tell he wanted too, just as he was convinced she had plenty more gush to give! In different circumstances, she would have been happy to carry on and see exactly how much more there was in her!

He picked her up and carried her across to the examination couch and sat her on top of it. His cock had brushed past her on route and she shuddered at its touch. He directed it inside her. It didn't need any guidance, as she was wet and wanting. Lou gasped with excitement and deep inside he slid. Struggling to contain herself she bit into his shoulder, trying to contain her delight. Oh, this really was what it was all about. This feeling of sheer pleasure discovered now in the most

VANILLA EXTRACT

inappropriate of places – pure brilliance!

Pushing herself into him, she felt every thrust. His arms were grabbing around her body, holding her up on the bed's edge. They could have gone on like this for the rest of the day, but time was not on their side. Lou had meetings soon and would have to get back to her desk. "As much as I really don't want to, I'm gonna have to go back," she told him. He understood. In some ways, it was a terrible time to stop, just as they were building their rhythm, but it also left them tingling and wanting more.

Mopping herself up with the paper towel conveniently located in the first aid room, she put herself back together, checking her clothes were intact, apart from the wet foot of course, which she couldn't do much about. Snake Hips rearranged himself too, making sure, as usual, that he looked immaculate. He explained that he didn't need to cum on this occasion but was excited about saving it for a full-on encounter with her. Lou looked forward to that!

Separately they made their way back to the office floor. To add to the illusion of being in different places, Lou went to the loo on the way back. He had been right. She still had a bladder full, so she hadn't peed down her leg earlier, which she was pleased to discover. Lou grabbed a coffee on route back and reappeared at the desk a few moments later. Snake Hips was at his computer, pretending to look busy, as she arrived. "Alright?" He asked as she sat down.

VANILLA EXTRACT

"Yeah, all good thanks. You?" she responded. He smiled cheekily at her above his screen. His eyes were sparkling more than normal. Lou tried her best not to look flustered while having a post-naughty glow all about her. Mmmmm, this felt like the start of an incredibly exciting adventure, she could tell. There was much fun to be had with Snake Hips, particularly now that line was firmly crossed.

VANILLA EXTRACT

Chapter 3 - Tim Sexy Policeman

A six-week adventure was about to begin with this rather delightful man. His courting technique was slightly different. It was through a professional social media site, set up for career progression and networking. (Who knew it could be used for this purpose too?) It appeared that their connection was through a mutual work friend of his, who just so happened to be Lou's neighbour.

"It seems we have someone in common," his approach began. At this particular time, that was all he needed. Lou was in the mood for meeting someone new and the timing was perfect. After some exchanging of pleasantries and getting to know each other online, they agreed to meet up. It was as easy as that!

When Tim came to meet her from work, a few things confirmed Lou had made the right choice in agreeing to meet him. Firstly, he stood way above her, even with her four-inch heels. Secondly, those eyes! Oh my goodness, they were amazing. Bright blue/green, they were piercing and had her captivated as soon she looked into them. Thirdly, when Lou asked if he wanted to go for a coffee or a drink, he actually gave a very definitive answer. "Oh

VANILLA EXTRACT

let's go for a proper drink, eh?" She loved his decisiveness. Too many times Lou had been faced with the more annoying answer of, "Well, what do you want to do?" Polite as men thought that was, Lou, like many other women, wanted the man to be masterful, and Tim certainly and rather refreshingly, was exactly that.

They went on to a bar in the Barbican area of London, where they sat and had a large glass of crisp and refreshing Pinot Grigio. With the conversation and outrageous flirting flowing freely, a full bottle followed as the intensity between them built. "So tell me Lou, are you wearing stockings, hold ups or tights under that suit?" She responded with an answer she had used a few times of late. "Well, I don't do tights." It seemed to provoke a reaction of increased interest. "Show me," Tim commanded. Lou obliged and lifted her skirt up where she sat in this crowded bar so that he could see the tops of her hold-ups. "I knew it! Let me take a picture of those sexy legs." Tim reached for his phone, as Lou flashed the lace-edged nylons. (The image would later become her profile picture elsewhere and attract lots of interest given it was taken in such a public place.)

"I want you to come back to my flat, so I can undress you, lay you on my bed and lick you till you cum all over my face. Then I want to slowly put my cock inside you and grind you so deep, you'll be screaming for me to stop." 'Bloody hell,' she thought. Instant turn on! The heat dial in her knickers just hit 200 degrees. She loved it when a guy knew his mind and told her so forthright. If only she could have clicked her fingers and be in his flat right there and then!

"I'm just up the road if you'd care to join me," Tim said. Impulsive and crazy at it was, Lou agreed. "Sure, fuck it! Why not?" They finished up their drinks there and then and made their way out of the bar. Arm in arm, they walked the ten-minute journey to his flat and half fell into it upon arrival.

The kissing started as soon they got inside. Lou was relieved to find he was a great kisser and she loved how he stooped over her, holding her face up as his tongue raced inside her mouth. It was ultra horny.

Tim's pad was very small but had everything he needed. His room consisted of a double bed, wardrobes and a sink. It was certainly basic. There was a shared bathroom and kitchen, not that Tim seemed the cooking type. With limited space, Lou could barely walk up the side of the bed when he offered to take her jacket, and that was the limit to his chivalry. His growing passion was evident in his trousers as he brushed past her to hang it up. Tempting as that was, Lou knew she couldn't give it any attention immediately. The wine had made its way straight to her bladder, so after a quick loo visit (and quick freshen up down there), Lou was ready for whatever this night was going to provide!

VANILLA EXTRACT

Lou was not disappointed as Tim proved he was a man of his word. When she returned, Tim pulled her in close to him. "You need to be naked so I can devour you." He began to unbutton Lou's blouse. Her breathing increased, deeper, heavier, as her nervous excitement overtook her body. It was beyond her control. He pushed the blouse off behind her and it dropped from her shoulders to the floor. (Being the end of a workday, she wasn't bothered that it would crease. She didn't have to go back to the office and look pristine.)

Lou's skirt was next. She decided to assist this time, given it was buttoned as well as zipped, and she didn't want it damaged in the heat of the moment. As she opened all the fastenings, it fell straight down, revealing her shapely legs in those hold-ups. "You've got a great set of pins," Tim said as his fingertips stroked the tops of the nylon. He then dropped to his knees so he could lick them. Lou's stomach somersaulted. Wow, what a turn on.

"Leave your shoes on and get on the bed," he instructed. Lou adored the dominance. He didn't have to say anything further. Lou got straight on and lay back, with legs dangling over the edge at her knees. Swiveling on the ground, he turned to where she was waiting in anticipation. Tim slid his arms underneath her thighs and raised them slightly in the air, then pulled his face into her pussy. Furiously slurping her in, his tongue was straight inside her,

VANILLA EXTRACT

lapping deep. Lou's back was arching before she caught her breath. 'Whoa,' she thought. 'This is crazy!' Lou loved the passion, but she didn't feel comfortable enough yet to cum. Whilst she was enjoying the intensity, she wasn't ready yet to explode. Perhaps sensing this Tim said, "I want you on my face. Let me get under you." Tim crawled onto the bed and turned onto his back. "I will look up at you as I take you." Lou moved up the bed and knelt either side of his face, as he'd suggested.

Lou felt a little self-conscious about her stomach, as many mothers do. It was the price women paid for producing new life and while Lou wouldn't change it for the world, she wasn't keen on her excess skin. She had once considered having a tummy tuck, until she learned exactly what was involved, not to mention the price. Instead, she embraced her stretch marks, as the certificate for life production that she had so rightfully earned. Ultimately it was only the media that told you not to be proud of them and that apparently you shouldn't look like you've had a baby, for some bizarre reason. Lou admired mothers that managed to get back to their pre-baby weight quickly. Kudos to them, particularly how they found the time to do anything non-baby-related was in itself a miracle!

Lou looked past her tummy, down at those amazing eyes staring up at her, and she watched as Tim did indeed take and take. She found she was able to relax now, although not really sure why. Maybe it was the build-up, the excitement and the nervous

VANILLA EXTRACT

adrenalin. Or maybe it was because Tim was enjoying her from deep within, but either way, Lou could feel her body erupting and there it was – a huge orgasm, straight into his mouth and it was obvious that he could not be happier! Neither could Lou, for that matter. She wasn't quite expecting that!

The reverberations were taking a while to subside as Lou climbed off Tim's mouth. His eyes were sparkling even more brightly now, almost like the energy of the orgasm had transferred directly to them. He was fuelled by her explosion and keen to continue.

Slowly Lou kissed him all over and was pleased to see him enjoying her tongue's sweet caress as she made her way down his chest in the direction of his erect penis. He was certainly ready for her. It was her first glimpse of what he was packing, and she wasn't disappointed. His cock was thick, with good girth and a lovely length. She was going to enjoy riding this as much as his face and probably more.

Once protection was in place, she slid down on top of him. Lou's body continued to flutter and tense. It was partly from the orgasm but now from the new sensation of feeling him deep inside her, and he felt so good! She began to grind down into him, rotating her hips to feel his cock touch every part of her vagina. "Oh, you ride me, baby!" Tim was still staring at her, his mouth slightly open in a paused smile of contentment, absorbing every manoeuvre and sensation. His hands slid onto her buttocks and

VANILLA EXTRACT

pulled her ever further down onto him, as deep as he could get. She could feel his nails slightly digging in, at first a sharp pain but then feeling quite pleasant as she continued this mounting.

The circular hip motions turned now to up and down, ever more erratically and forcefully. Lou found herself slamming against him as they fucked harder. Sweat was forming on her back as she worked his cock more vigorously. Tim was lifting her bum up in the air with every thrust as they slapped back into each other. Both smiling, both laughing, this was incredibly sexy.

With ease, Tim reached up and pushed Lou onto the bed now. "Get on your knees!" Lou was straight to it. They both wanted this as much as each other. The mirrored wardrobe provided the best view for them both to watch Tim pounding the living daylights out of Lou, and they both enjoyed the show. This was brilliant - so very hot indeed!

Tim moved back and pulled Lou to the edge of the bed. His feet now firmly on the ground, he could penetrate her even deeper, if that was even possible. It transpired that it was! While giving it to her from behind, Tim slapped Lou's arse with such force that she gasped in pain. She had never experienced this before, and she wasn't quite sure if she liked it. Her instant reaction was to pull away, turn and probably punch him, but in these circumstances, that didn't quite feel right. She decided to let it go, but because she didn't particularly want him to do that again,

VANILLA EXTRACT

she shouted, "Do that again and I'll hit back!" It was enough of a deterrent.

Tim abided by her wishes and continued to pump her until he could pump no more. His body was ready now to indulge in the prize he had worked so hard for. "Oh fuck. I'm gonna come!" Frantically he whipped off the condom as quickly as he could and cast it to the floor. Tim came all over Lou's pert, and now very sweaty awaiting bottom.

Both now collapsed on the bed - Tim to her side and Lou onto her front to avoid any spillages or stains. There they laughed about their encounter until Tim found some tissue and cleaned her up. It certainly had been a good 'meet' or was that 'meat,' even if she did have a Tim-sized handprint on her right buttock.

After they had both separately showered, they went out for some food and spent the rest of the night together at Tim' place, where rounds two and three occurred, with copious amounts of red wine, before she trundled off to work the next morning.

Lou was to become a regular visitor and pushed a few boundaries with him that she hadn't anticipated. These included becoming a bit of a star on the site's webcam facility, where they would regularly perform live sex to their awaiting audience. Viewers would have their own cameras on and comment in real time for them both to read.

VANILLA EXTRACT

Lou and Tim became quite obsessive about their popularity and could see how many were watching them. It became a bit of a game, making sure their show was getting the highest volumes of voyeurs. Lou didn't consider at the time what a security risk this was – not really knowing who was watching and what they were potentially doing with any screen shots or recording they took. (Lesson learned and never repeated after her time with this sexy policeman.)

Tim also introduced Lou to 'the wand'. Some would say it could put a spell on you and it certainly had some magical powers, but it wasn't made of wood and it had to be plugged it in. The results were mind-blowing as Lou found out when Tim had her straddled across his right thigh, and he held the wand in place on her clitoris. At first, it was too intense, and she wriggled about erratically because she could not take the force. After a while, Lou learned to relax into it and 'ride' the powerful waves she felt within herself, not even aware that pre-cum was rolling down her legs and over Tim's thigh, saturating the bed below.

Lou found herself more in control and rotated her hips in a circular motion, grinding against the toy and Tim's thigh. The feeling inside her was getting stronger and stronger and she was beginning to enjoy it rather than fight it. More pushing down onto it now, she was ready to let go. Lou gripped onto Tim's thigh, as the crescendo was imminent. Her nails dug in deep into his flesh as she reached

VANILLA EXTRACT

her peak and felt the release explode all over him. OMG, this was fucking huge – like a million electrodes had sprung into action at the same time and after the intense shock, the energy was now flowing through her. Lou was tingling all over and it didn't seem to be slowing down any. The shudders were deep, consuming her entire body, and they continued for an eternity, it seemed.

Tim was smiling up at her, despite the gouges in his thigh. He could tell exactly what she had just experienced and was looking very pleased with himself for having introduced Lou to this whole new level of excitement. She had a feeling she wasn't the first lady to have broken her wand 'cherry' under Tim's direction, not that it made any difference to her. She was thrilled to have reached this new euphoria, despite the drenched bed she left below her.

Another time Tim seemed very keen to introduce one of his other female friends to their play, but Lou wasn't quite sure this was what she wanted. He suggested she would be tied up and waiting for them at Tim's when Lou finished work. She would be their muse, to do with what Lou wanted, but Lou felt uncomfortable with this arrangement. At that stage, Lou would quite have fancied having a spare man involved in their play, or alternatively, she wanted to be the one tied up and played with. Either way, it just didn't feel right, so she declined this offer. Tim appeared quite upset that she didn't want to explore

VANILLA EXTRACT

this opportunity and it sparked the end of their six-week adventure.

Lou learned a lot during her short spell with Tim, about what she liked, what her comfort zones were, and with this knowledge, she felt her confidence grow. Lou wondered when looking back and once she was more experienced in this new world she had immersed herself in, whether she should revisit Tim. It would be interesting to show him just how much she had developed since their encounters at the beginning of her journey of self-discovery.

Lou speculated on how he would react if she shared with him some of her more recent encounters, for instance, when she attended a fetish event in London. It was a brilliant night with lots of beautiful people, all appreciating the effort that was made with their outfits. Lou herself adorned a latex ensemble. It hugged in all the right places and had parts cut out of the rubber material quite clearly showing her lady parts. Such had Lou's confidence grown that she was happily talking to new friends with her dignity exposed for all to see.

A gorgeous young Sicilian man called Dani had caught her eye and she could feel the instant chemistry between them. He was a hairdresser and budding IT student, who happened to play the guitar and sing in a band. He was hot. Lou couldn't wait to have him later but was enjoying the flirting and getting to know him.

VANILLA EXTRACT

As the evening went on, their paths crossed a few times, each time they stayed together longer and chatted more. At one point, his drink was knocked slightly, and a few drops of it poured onto Lou's forearm. She held it out to him and said, "You need to lick that up." Dani had already read her mind before she spoke and was on the case. Jokingly, Lou pointed down to her groin, and said, "Some spilt there too." In the middle of the dance floor, Dani knelt down before her and began to devour her wanting pussy. People around them began to watch. She absolutely adored it – the sensation of him licking and the voyeuristic stares. It was brilliant. Lou loved moments like this.

After some more intimate tasting, Dani stood up and kissed her deeply. It was electric and super horny. They had no choice but to go and find a room and have each other entirely. Phew – hot, hot, hot!

This was how Lou was to progress and grow into her sexuality, albeit after quite a few experiences along the way. She was sure Tim Sexy Policeman would approve and wondered if one day they would share some of her stories (and his) in the future – possibly naked and straddled across his thigh once more.

VANILLA EXTRACT

Chapter Four - Tattooed Temptation

For what must have been close to a year Lou and Tattooed Temptation (Brandon) had spoken at various times online but both had taken a back seat to life, new adventures, and different partners. They had a connection many moons ago but had never gone further with it, for whatever reason. But today was different. Today Lou had nothing to do. Despite still feeling a bit low after a head cold, it was a bright Saturday and she didn't want to waste it. Her children were with their father for the weekend, so there was no real reason to stay at home alone. What's more was that she was feeling horny and had an itch that needed scratching.

When he messaged back, Lou began to get excited. There was some caution too though, as usual, when a meet was beginning to look like a possibility. Her immediate reaction to his suggestion of hooking up filled her with a little nervousness and dread. Giving herself a get out clause, she messaged back saying how she had been feeling a little under the weather but would see how she felt later. "Oh come on," he said, "what else are you going to be doing?" He had a good point. Suddenly her sniffles of this morning seemed to miraculously disappear as the thoughts of meeting this young buck began to grow.

VANILLA EXTRACT

There were a few hours to kill before the scheduled time to meet. Fortunately, Lou had completed all the preparation beforehand – shaved her legs, armpits and trimmed down below. Well, it was always good to be prepared, and this time it had paid off. This allowed her to take her time with her make-up and hair straightening. Because she knew she had plenty of time, she relaxed and got into the flow. She chose her outfit. It was tried and tested - casual but classy. Her skin-tight black leggings showed the natural curves of her legs, black strappy vest top under a cream crotched loose fitting jumper allowed her colourful back tattoos just ever so slightly to show through. The killer five-inch heeled boots set the outfit off, and now it was complete with just enough suggestion of her sluttier side.

As usual, Lou chose a public location for the first meeting. This gave her the security of knowing she could escape if need be, particularly if:

a) He had a screw loose,
b) His pictures were taken years ago before the hair fell out and the pounds had piled themselves on,
c) Or if they just didn't hit it off

These were all experiences she had endured at some stage recently, but she felt tonight was going to be different. She certainly hoped so.

The pub was conveniently situated next to a tube station on the Central Line, but also with good road

VANILLA EXTRACT

links as she was driving. It also just so happened to have a hotel situated right next door, which might come in handy. Well, it was always good to be prepared and to have options in case the meet went exceptionally well.

He was running a little late. It gave her time to park up, and cheekily check out if the hotel had any rooms. She was in luck – there were five rooms available should this social meeting turn into something much more. This was information she would keep to herself for now – handy to have up her sleeve.

Lou was starting to feel a little nervous as she walked into the pub. Fortunately, she knew the layout from being a customer many years before. Trying to stay focussed and carry off the nonchalant air, boot heels clipping the tiled floor, she headed straight to the toilets. It turned out that the nerves were taking hold and she didn't need the loo anyway. After a quick check of her make-up, tidy of her hair and re-applying of her lip-gloss, she was good to go.

As he would still be a little while, Lou messaged him to ask what drink he would like. With that in mind, she made her way to the bar and placed the order. She would stick with a white wine spritzer for now, as she wasn't sure if she would be driving home or not – best to leave her options open!

Leaving the bar with the drinks, she spied him out of the corner of her eye walking towards her. Taller

VANILLA EXTRACT

than she remembered from his profile, Brandon's hair was shaved at the sides and longer on top. It was more ginger than strawberry blonde she thought and his eyes were a bright shiny green. His youthful face had a cheeky grin and she could tell instantly that he was full of fun and mischief.

He was dressed casually, having come from seeing friends in London Bridge that afternoon, and he appeared to be ultra-relaxed. "Oh you look great," he said as he reached over and kissed her on the cheek. "Thank you," she responded and gave him his pint. She guided him to a table and so the conversation began.

Although it had been a while since they had talked at any length online, tonight was like meeting for the very first time – and not just in the physical sense. He had a great personality and matching sense of humour. The pair of them were chatting and laughing so much that they were almost late for the table she had booked earlier.

As they headed over to the restaurant area, he placed his hand on her bottom and gave it a brazen squeeze. It was something she had not expected, but she didn't mind. In fact, she quite liked it. They were then shown to their table, where he took the seat right next to her instead of opposite. Initially, this felt a little odd for her; a little like her space was being invaded, but he had already put her at ease and she really didn't mind. As the conversation continued, she soon got used to it and she was pleased there was no barrier between them.

Putting his hand on her thigh, he asked her to describe her best, and worst, sexual encounters. That was easy. She started in reverse. The most recent worst sexual experience was a recent 'charity fuck' as she had so eloquently put it. It had been with a man from work, albeit based in a different office. They had chatted on internal messaging systems for a while and flirted more recently. Role-play online had ensued to the point where they both found sexual gratification separately. This was before they had even met in person. When they did finally meet, they had drinks and dinner and somehow ended back at his hotel, by which time she felt it was too late to turn back. Nothing was against her will, but Lou felt they had sex just for the sake of it. Well, that was how she viewed it. He may well have felt differently. The sooner she put this episode behind her, the better, she openly admitted to the lovely Brandon.

The best sexual encounter recently was when Lou had met someone for dinner. It was a man she had known in a work capacity for some time. He was a supplier and they had shared a few lunch appointments before, but a dinner date was very different to the norm. When it came to the evening meeting, there had been an underlying passion so strong that they had not made it to ordering food. Instead, they had found themselves abandoning the restaurant, jumping in a taxi and having a much

VANILLA EXTRACT

more exciting feast in a local hotel. The spontaneity, the knowing and the sheer excitement had led to a steamy sex session that neither of them had anticipated for that evening.

How funny that she could be recalling this to someone she just met, but such was the level of comfort she felt with him. Brandon felt like an old friend and they were having an open, very honest and humorous conversation.

Brandon was toying with her now. "Oh, so that was a ploy? Do you want to leave with me now then and forget the food?" It was almost too cliché now for her to say yes. She did inform him that she had checked out the hotel next door, just in case - not that she was being presumptuous. Although she did have an overnight bag in her boot, of course, which she enjoyed telling him about too. She even offered him her toothbrush, given he had only expected to be having a social and not a passionate encounter. "You have protection too?" he asked. Of course she did. Whilst she had never been a scout, she was a mature woman, who had spent some years of her career in contingency planning. She was always prepared!

They did order food, and it was just as well they did, for they were both in for a very long and exhausting night ahead. With a little vanity thrown in, the dishes they chose to eat were not too filling as both didn't wish to appear bloated at the time when they became naked and revealed all to each other.

VANILLA EXTRACT

The sparks were flying now as the electricity between them cranked up a few notches. Feelings of naughtiness and lust all rolled into one, Lou decided it would be best to make a quick visit to the toilet before they left the pub. She needed to go and didn't want to be peeing in the hotel room for him to hear. They weren't anywhere near that stage yet of urinating in front of each other! That would be embarrassing enough, but what if she passed wind too. There would be no coming back from that, apart from having to laugh it off, which, in fairness, with him, she probably could. She'd prefer not to put herself in that position just in case!

Before heading next door to the hotel, Brandon pulled her in close and said they needed to go to the supermarket. Unless the protection she brought was for the larger lad, they would have to invest in some more that would fit him. 'Wowza,' she thought and wondered if he was winding her up. Just how big was he down there? Or was this just a joke? Either way, it started her thinking about what was going on inside his trousers exactly and what delights would she have to contend with later?

As well as the large condoms, Brandon bought some beers and some luxury vanilla ice cream. Her mind was racing now. What exactly was he planning with that ice cream - dessert or accessory? She was looking forward to finding out which.

The hotel receptionist looked rather bemused when they came to make their late reservation. She had a

VANILLA EXTRACT

knowing look on her face as she took their details down. This was not the first time a horny, fully charged couple had stood before her wanting a room with such urgency, nor would it be the last.

Armed with their new purchases, they made their way to the lift to take them up to their floor and this is where it became even more heated. As he followed her into the lift, he came right up behind her and pushed his groin into her back. It sent shivers straight up her spine to her neck, as he pushed her hair to one side and planted his first kiss there. The doors closed behind them. His breath was hot, and his lips were moist. She loved this intensity. It was incredibly exciting.

He turned her around to face him and then it began. There was an electrifying buzz between them. Tongues tangled, hands groped, bags bashed; it was only short moments before the lift door opened at level three.

Smiling, they rearranged their attire then raced to find room 327. Typically it was almost at the other end of the seemingly never-ending corridor. Fumbling to swipe the door fob, they managed to barge into the room and straight into each other. Slipping the bags onto the bed, they wanted first to explore each other's mouths before anything else.

The kissing was incredibly good. His tongue was all over hers, and it was making her body twitch from deep within. Saliva was in abundance - more than

VANILLA EXTRACT

she was used to and her face was becoming wet. Wiping it off she felt a bit rude. She hoped this didn't insult him. Brandon laughed, "Ah yes, I am a bit of a slobbery kisser. It's just that my tongue is massive," and with that, he pulled away and poked it out to show her. No way! It was absolutely enormous, like having a soft pink spade hidden inside a hot, wet cave. He flicked it up and down in the air just to confirm, and her thoughts became instantly erotic, as she imagined what that would feel like all over and inside her.

Brandon moved the bags from the bed to the side and offered her a drink. How very civilised, Lou thought. Beer it was! They both took a swig from their bottles, but the alcohol wasn't really what either of them wanted right now. Swiftly putting them on the side, they came back to each other. He began to take off his T-shirt, and she kissed his nipples. Finally, she was able to see his tattoos close up. Until now they'd only ever been small online pictures, and it was always best to examine artwork up close. She intended to study it all directly, with her tongue.

As Brandon stood with his arms up, Lou licked his chest from his left side across to the right and then back to the middle. He slung his top across the room and let her continue. She was making her way down from his chest to the top of his trousers. He smelled and tasted great. Lingering on his trouser waistband, she slipped her tongue across the top

VANILLA EXTRACT

from side to side, just dipping below, and sending shivers deeply through him to his core.

Unbuckling his belt, Lou helped his trousers fall to the floor, as she focussed on the bulge in his pants. As with his tongue, she didn't think his cock would disappoint her either. Brandon's solid penis was ready for her. She rubbed it ever so gently through the material before her hand caressed his ball sack and she gripped a little more firmly. She dropped to her knees so she could indulge in a closer inspection as she reached inside his pants to free this swollen beast.

Easing his pants over his erection, Lou pushed them downwards but wasn't concerned if they made it to the floor, or if he wanted to step out of them. Her full attention was required here, and he needed to be inside her mouth. As usual, she rarely went straight in for the kill. She liked to tease and make her man want her more. Nuzzling into his groin, she licked slowly. Brandon tasted clean, despite being out all day. He must have had a freshen-up along the way somewhere. Nibbling his sensitive area, she moved her tongue along and to his right thigh and began to lick. A gasp escaped him. Oh, he liked this and it made her feel good about being in control. Gently biting and tasting his skin, she moved across to his left thigh. Similar teasing continued until he could take no more. It was time for her to take him in her mouth.

Wrapping her hand around his huge cock, Lou eased her mouth down towards him. Brandon was rock

VANILLA EXTRACT

hard and slightly dribbling on top there. She took great pleasure in licking off the pre-cum. It was tasteless but sticky and he found it erotic that she was consuming the fluid his body so readily released. Swallowing, she moved down his shaft with her tongue, gently licking up and down. He wanted her to take him all in, but she was happily teasing and he was enjoying the anticipation.

"Let's move back to the bed," he whispered. Lou was keen to please, and he wanted to savour this moment fully and preferably on his back. Brandon laid himself down, managing to escape his pants and now completely naked. Climbing onto the bed between his legs, she grabbed his penis with her left hand and she began to caress it with her tongue. Slowly licking and looking up at him, it was becoming even more responsive. She slid it into her mouth and was moving up and down, flicking her wrist with every motion, and it was obvious he loved it. He released some gentle sighs and moans in the heat of the moment as she got to work.

Many men had previously told her that her oral skills were second to none and her online verifications certainly echoed that. "Oh my days, oral skills like never before," from one satisfied partner and, "She seriously knows how to please. No idea what she does with that tongue of hers, but please, please, keep on doing it." Of course, she did keep doing it too, much to Brandon's delight.

VANILLA EXTRACT

Getting ready perform her special form of magic on him, she focussed on the end of his cock. Always such a sensitive area, she had learned to lick with pressure. All men seemed to enjoy this, but it could get very intense for them – too intense at times. His back was arching. ("Yes!" she said to herself as she secretly punched the air in her mind. She loved making a man arch his back. It meant she was doing it right and, more often than not, better than they'd ever had before.)

"Holy fuck! What are you doing down there?" he shrieked as his body released and tensed once more. This only encouraged her to continue to inflict more pleasure upon him. Again she pressed down with her tongue. Gripping the sides of the bed, he was utterly in her control, gasping as she repeated the process. "Too much! Too much," he screamed out. She eased off and began to gently nibble his inner thighs to allow him to calm down. His back sank into the bed and he began to breathe more regularly. She was feeling a bit relieved too – she certainly didn't want him shooting his load just yet.

As Brandon drifted into this new sensation, the soft caressing with her mouth made him smile sweetly. "I don't know what you were doing there, but it was bloody crazy. God that felt good! It's only right I give you something back. I want you wriggling and squirming just as much as I did!" Lou beamed with excitement as he pulled her close and then threw her down on the bed next to him.

VANILLA EXTRACT

Now it was about to get interesting for her. Time to see what tricks that massive tongue could perform. He had been so lost in his own pleasure that he didn't realise Lou still had her boots on! "Let's get these off for starters," he said as he reached down and unzipped her boots, casting them aside. The leggings were next. He crawled up her body, so his head hovered a few centimetres above her for the entire journey from her feet. Gripping the top of her leggings with his teeth, he gently began to pull them down. "Mmmm, I like," he said as he saw what was now revealed. Of course, she had put on some beautiful underwear. Tonight's treat was a matching black lace two set which fit like a glove. (The bra fit snuggly and gave her enough lift to demonstrate there was a cleavage in there somewhere to be displayed, without pushing her breasts so far up and out that they would only be a disappointment once released of their support! The knickers were pretty and gave no Visual Panty Line [VPL], which was a result.)

Brandon's hands now came in to play, as it was too difficult to carry that manoeuvre through to fruition with just his mouth. He peeled her leggings down to her feet and off, taking her delicate socks off in the same sweeping movement. Lying there in the lace French knickers, she couldn't wait. She pulled off her jumper and was struggling with the vest when he came to assist. "Let me," he suggested and helped her out of final clothes.

VANILLA EXTRACT

Pausing for a moment, he admired her. "Oh you look good enough to eat," he smiled the biggest of smiles and began to devour. Starting with her mouth, he charged his 'spade' inside. His tongue was as wet as before and he was making it very moist between her legs. Tender yet masterful, he moved down to her neck, gaging instantly just how sensitive she was. He lingered longer, kissing her just below each ear, nuzzling in so she could feel his hot breath. It felt good and was making her hips grind involuntarily.

Next, on to her shoulders, he slipped both bra straps down with his teeth and began to kiss her collarbones. While she was enjoying the delectable attention, she was also eager to assist. She reached behind and undid her bra, exposing her breasts for his attention. An animalistic growl escaped him as he went straight in and began to chew on her tits, forcing them into his mouth. There was a mixture of passion and gentle teasing all wrapped into one as he then went back to caressing her skin with his wet tongue. She felt that he wanted to be rough with her, but he didn't know her well enough and he didn't want to make her feel uncomfortable. Either way, she adored the mixed sensations she was experiencing.

The feeling of his teeth gently biting on her erect nipples was sending currents straight to her clitoris. Being intrinsically linked, any breast action was being replicated in between her legs and she began to moan. This man knew exactly what he was doing.

VANILLA EXTRACT

"You alright there hon.?" he laughed. "Oh god yes," she replied and continued to enjoy his touch.

It was only a moment later that he was licking her stomach and lowering himself down her body. Onto her knickers, he began licking the delicate lace instead of removing them. They were becoming wet now from both sides, and he could taste her. "Mmm, you taste good," as he pulled them to the side and slid his huge tongue inside her glistening pussy. She was ready but still let out a gasp as he plunged inside. It felt amazing and that was before Brandon unleashed his true tongue skills – at which point, Lou didn't know quite what had hit her.

He pulled her knickers down and off over one leg. It was enough to allow the full access he required. Flicking rapidly on her clit, his tongue was like a machine. Intensity like the 'wand' adult toy she had shared with Tim Sexy Policeman, this was difficult to keep under control. Lou's legs began to shake, her pussy was convulsing, and she was getting wetter and wetter with each rub of his tongue. She knew from previous experiences, and the wand, that she would have to relax into this to be able to experience it at its fullest.

Breathing deeply and enjoying every intense wave, Lou felt she was gaining control again. She anticipated the cyclic rhythm and rode it. She was close to orgasm when he suddenly stopped the momentum. "The ice-cream!" he bellowed with a cheeky grin. Getting up swiftly, he rummaged

VANILLA EXTRACT

through the carrier bag, then came rushing back to the bed with the somewhat warmer container. With no freezer facilities, it had proceeded to melt, but it was still cold enough to do the trick.

"Aha, what do we have here then?" Brandon asked as he removed the lid and scooped up some ice cream with two fingers. Mostly fluid, it was dripping on the bed as he moved towards her. "Very creamy indeed," he said and then spread her labia with the other hand. She instantly flinched as he placed the chilly, sodden fingers inside her. Her already wet pussy was now tingling with the cold and it was about to drop a few more degrees. He took a deep breath and blew cold air onto her clit. She shuddered and was just acclimatising when he plunged his hot soggy tongue back on her. "Fuck," she expelled! The transition from freezing to heated was instant. It was a complete shock but incredibly amazing too. Again, again, again, she was hoping.

Brandon wasn't easing off any. Just as she was getting used to the heat, the ice cream was back in play. Alternating between the different temperatures and textures, her body was confused with the different sensations, but loving every moment. 'Tingly, tingly,' she thought to herself and wondered how many times he was going to repeat this. Each time it brought her closer to release. Finally, it didn't take much to send her over the edge, with his relentless forceful stroking of her clit with his tongue. The continual rubbing and changes of hot and cold were more than she could handle, despite

VANILLA EXTRACT

having felt in control earlier. "Yes, yes, yes, I'm cumming," she squealed as she let go. It was huge and she felt instant relief and release, not to mention a large, sticky wet patch growing beneath her on the bed. Wow – so very, very good!

Lou's body convulsed as it calmed down slowly. Watching her shudder, Brandon moved up to kiss her deeply. It felt delightful and tasted so, particularly with the ice cream remnants in his saliva. It was a mixture of vanilla and her own juices, and while she had enjoyed every feeling, she had a quick pang of doubt about the whole scenario. In the back of her mind, her practical thoughts kicked in. She couldn't help wonder if this delicious episode would mean a visit to the chemist would be necessary in a day or so for the thrush cream!

Continuing to kiss her, his cock was sword-like and rubbed against her body. It was obvious where he was going next. "I hope you've got one of your super-size condoms ready," she said, more to ensure he was clear that she wanted him to wear one. She had no need to worry. He was on the case. "Coming right up, my lady," he joked, as he made sure they were both protected.

Lou was excited to see how the sex would be with this lovely young man. He had the looks, the banter, a brilliant sense of humour and the tongue skills of a true master. Could his cock be equally as satisfying or more? She would be over the moon if

VANILLA EXTRACT

he truly was the entire package (so to speak) and was about to find out.

Smiling, he resumed the position on top of her as she lay on the bed. Slowly, he placed his penis directly above her and slid it in, maintaining eye contact the entire time. It fit perfect if a little too big, but neither of them seemed to mind. Once they established just how good this felt for them both, the fireworks began.

Who knew that he would have the stamina of a Spartan and that she would go home the next day barely able to walk straight? She was not disappointed in the slightest when he got going! It was deep. It was fast. It was hard. She savoured each stab of his huge, solid penis. She dug her nails into his buttocks with every thrust, and this turned him on even more. It helped her pull him into her even further, not that he needed any assistance.

Every position was tried. Every position felt unbelievable. They were well matched sexually, and that was evident by the mess they made all over the hotel room. 'Thank goodness this wasn't at my house,' she thought. The duvet would have been saturated, not to mention the mattress. It would have taken ages to clear up and a few days of drying out!

For hours they continued to trash that room, till the point where they noticed it was getting light outside. How did that happen? Both of them came a

VANILLA EXTRACT

number of times, and at the point where they were drenched, covered in sweat and bodily fluids, they decided to take a breather. "How would you like to update your portfolio online?" he asked her. Of course, she would love to take new photos, and he apparently had an eye for it. 'Splendid – bring it on,' she thought.

Brandon told her to put her boots back on and lean against the wall. "Pretend someone is taking you from behind," he directed her. Naturally, Lou obliged, and he happily snapped away with her phone. "You look amazing," he said, and she was happy with how her figure looked, but she was less pleased with displaying her private parts quite so publicly. Lou was of the thinking that less is more. She didn't particularly like showing all her 'secrets' to random strangers who may copy and do who knows what with her images. So, slipping her panties back on, they tried again and she was over the moon with the results.

Brandon certainly did know what he was doing with the camera. "Well I'm a bloke, and I know what blokes like." This seemed obvious enough, and of course, he was right. They decided to experiment to see how many 'likes' she received on her profile compared with him as a single male, using exactly the same shots. The results were phenomenal. Within seconds she began to receive interest. Men clicked to show they liked the pictures and then began to send messages to her profile. In fact, it didn't stop – for the next four days, her inbox was

VANILLA EXTRACT

inundated. It was quite ridiculous. On the flip side, Brandon received just one like for one of the same photos!

After their interval for photography and social research, they resumed their naked encounters back under the covers this time. It proved less frantic as they were both tired and a little tender too! There was hardly anything they could do with or to each other without causing discomfort. They decided to call it a day and snuggle up instead. Sleep was a far better option and they had certainly both earned it! Assuming the spoons position, they both dozed for a few hours until it was time to part and go about their normal Sunday routines.

After sharing a shower, Lou dropped him off at the local tube station before she drove home. They agreed that they definitely needed to see each other again and very soon, preferably as soon as their respective sore bits healed. Lou desperately needed sleep, and a full all-over massage might have helped after the workout he had given her. Aching as she was, she wondered how bad it would be over the next two days when the body would let her know just how much effort they had put into the overnight experience! There was always something satisfying about aching after a good session, and she knew she would be smiling knowingly with every painful twinge.

It would only be a few days before she met Brandon again (and again and again as it transpired). Lou was so pleased she took the plunge that first time.

VANILLA EXTRACT

He became a great friend as well as a fantastic lover, and she knew she was in for a treat every time she led herself unto her Tattooed Temptation!

VANILLA EXTRACT

Chapter Five - Chicken Dinner

This was one of Lou's less than great adventures from an online sex site. She took the opportunity to view it as a life lesson for future reference and, also, as the source of much amusement - after the event, of course. Living through it at the time was quite a different experience.

The problem, as she discovered first-hand, is that when you are bombarded by so many messages from men online, you can overlook some of the minor details (and major details too, as she soon found out). Compounding that with the ratio of males to females being so out of balance, it was easy for women to sometimes talk quite happily to lots of men, without realising who exactly was behind the pictures and the chat at the other end.

His photos looked great, although she surmised afterwards that they had been edited with some sort of fade filter. Lou found the banter between them quite funny. He had a good sense of humour, and she spent quite a few hours chatting and laughing with him online. They planned a social meet in the next week or so. He was very keen to cook for her, and they discussed what that meal should be. His speciality was a roast dinner, and of the choices he gave her, she opted for chicken. Lou was looking

VANILLA EXTRACT

forward to the idea of a roast dinner without having to cook it or have to tidy up after it. What a treat! He would even prepare a dessert too. If she brought the chocolate, he would melt it over the fresh strawberries he would buy that day. It all sounded rather delicious. What could go wrong?

Leaving from work, Lou plugged his address into her satnav. It was 22 miles away and she would be there within the hour - London traffic permitting. As she drew closer to the destination, she noticed the residential area was very lively with children playing in the park and many people returning home from their busy days. This was all very pleasant.

Lou was less than impressed though when the guidance brought her to the final address. The three-storey flats were dilapidated and scaffolding surrounded them entirely. Making her way to number 27, she had to step over the dust sheets, past the decorators with their wet paint, and up the stairs. This did feel like a bit of an obstacle course, not made any easier by her four-inch heels she had worn to work all day. Lou felt quite a sense of achievement when she reached his door, and she hadn't even rung the bell yet. Wafts of the cooking roast greeted her. It was a moment she should have savoured, given it was probably the highlight of the evening.

After that, Lou's night became progressively more awkward, pretty much from the point of him

VANILLA EXTRACT

opening the door to the moment she managed to escape back through it again.

Lou managed to conceal her shock as the man who greeted her stood at a grand height of approximately four feet and eight inches tall. This was not quite what she had expected! If she had no conscience at all, she would have left immediately, but she could smell the chicken and knew he had gone to a lot of effort. It would have been mean to have made her excuses at the door there and then and left swiftly, despite her desperately wanting to.

They exchanged a kiss on the cheek as he welcomed her to his man-cave. Inside Lou wondered, 'What the hell am I doing here?' as he guided her to the lounge area. "I won't be a moment," he said, as he went back to the kitchen, allowing her to relax while she waited. This gave her an opportunity to have a look around and it didn't get any better.

'Each to their own,' she thought as she perused the multitude of Star Wars memorabilia. Every shelf had figurines all set in particular positions, as they were no doubt fighting a war in some imaginary sci-fi world. An episode of *Star Trek - Next Generation* was just coming to an end on his television as he wandered back in the room, looking a little embarrassed. "Oh, let's turn that off. I'm sure you don't want to watch that." Well, that much was true, but what was more apparent to Lou was that she didn't want to be here at all.

VANILLA EXTRACT

"What would you like to watch?" he asked before he retreated back to the stove. Given she knew exactly how this meeting was going to turn out, she opted for an episode of a mediocre soap opera she often found herself watching at this time of the day. There was no point in getting behind in the story for the sake of this disappointing encounter!

What she also realised, while sitting here in a stranger's flat, in an area she didn't know, was that she hadn't thought this through whatsoever. In fact, she had been very stupid. No one knew she was here. If something were to go horribly wrong, then who would know? Note to self: let someone know who she was meeting and where. It was a matter of personal security and one that should be taken seriously. This could be via a telephone check-in call or messaging a friend the address and contact details. It was always better to be safe than sorry, as the saying goes.

When he returned to the sitting room, he offered Lou a glass of the white wine she had brought. Fortunately, as it transpired on this occasion, she was driving and had the perfect excuse a) not to drink more than one glass and b) get away swiftly, both of which would come into play as soon as possible. She accepted a small glass and offered him a hand in the kitchen. "No, no, no," he said. It was all under control and just a few minutes later, he brought out the dinner he had so caringly prepared for her.

VANILLA EXTRACT

He handed her the tray with her dinner on. Lou then realised there was no table to sit at. Instead, the two-seater sofa would be where they both ate their food. This was not at all ideal, and she always thought you should eat sitting upright, particularly as this sofa was tiny. Elbows would be clashing, she was sure, and she preferred to have no physical contact whatsoever.

The conversation wasn't exactly flowing either. It was more like dripping in a Japanese water torture kind of way. The main topics he wanted to cover were his health conditions and problems with maintaining the flat they were both now squashed up into. 'The sties in both of his eyes did look sore,' she thought, as he continued with his saga. He went on to tell her how difficult it was proving to have his washing machine repaired, which was really annoying him, particularly as it was such a long and drawn out process for this seemingly easy task. ('Really?' she wondered, trying to look interested as she wished the time away.)

After taking her tray back to the kitchen, he asked if she wanted more wine. Lou declined graciously and then thought it was time she broke the news to him. Staying for dessert was not going to happen. (This did remind her of a colleague at work who had a blind date and ended up having dinner with him, despite not fancying him in the slightest. Her ordeal lasted almost five hours because she was too kind and didn't want to come across as uninterested!)

VANILLA EXTRACT

There was no way Lou was going through something like that! Action was required, and it had to be now.

"I'm really sorry, but I won't be staying for the strawberries," she told him. It was a difficult line to deliver, particularly as most of the conversation was awkward enough. But he was not surprised in the slightest. However, he was disappointed. That much was obvious in the way his body crumpled up as she spoke. His whole demeanour changed and he looked deflated. "I'm just not feeling we have any chemistry," Lou continued. It was harsh, but it was true. His response was not quite what she expected. "Why do they all say that?" he asked and wandered back into the kitchen. 'Ouch! Well, that could have gone better,' she thought as she started to collect up her things. Fortunately that only really meant her bag and coat, so she had no excuse to stay any longer.

"I suppose you won't message me anymore now either," he stated as she joined him in the kitchen. "Of course I will," Lou lied blatantly. She would still for a while, but not for too much longer. This much she knew for sure. There was no sexual connection and given they had met on a sex site; there really wasn't much point was there?

He handed her the chocolate she had brought for melting and suggested she kept it. Being female and being offered chocolate, she naturally took it and put it in her bag. She would forfeit the wine. He

VANILLA EXTRACT

could have that for cooking the dinner (which had been OK as far as roast chicken dinners go).

Another kiss on the cheek farewell and then Lou hurried back to her car. It was possibly the longest couple of hours of her life, which she would never get back again. But in some respects, she had learned a lot. For one: to read the profiles in more detail. Two: to make sure she checked just how tall they were before agreeing to meet. Three: (and possibly the most safety-aware of them all,) to make sure someone else knew where she would be. However good the promise of a cooked meal was, it was not worth risking her safety, even if the force was not particularly strong with this one!

VANILLA EXTRACT

Chapter Six - Impale Me!

The photos she uploaded to her online profile recently were an instant success. Over 400 messages in her inbox in the next 24 hours and Lou made it to 3rd position in the hottest pictures listing for the entire site. It was her personal best and she didn't mind sharing the good news with Brandon. 'Well done that man,' she thought, initially. He certainly had an eye for what men wanted to see.

After a while and a few more days, the newly found fame became a bit of a burden to Lou. Day two and another 300 new approaches with the same old banter were becoming tedious. Without being conceited, she found the "You're fit," or "Hi, how are you?" approach a little lacking in imagination and charm; made even worse when it was incorrect grammatically with 'your fit', for example, which did nothing but niggle her.

The Impaler's approach was altogether different and very direct. Lou immediately liked him. "Hi. I'm Andy. I think you are beautiful and your pictures are amazing. I'm going to a club night on Thursday and I would like you to be my guest. Please message me if you fancy coming along." Well, that made a refreshing change. He was complimentary, non-

VANILLA EXTRACT

pushy and a somewhat of a gentleman. How could she resist?

Lou struck up a conversation with him and became 'friends' on the site. Andy was very easy to talk with and when she looked through his profile images, she was not disappointed with what he looked like either. He was muscly, heavily tattooed and very well endowed. She noticed that he had looked at her profile a number of times, and after reading his and seeing his tattoos, she decided to look at his verifications. They were all very positive with a few ladies remarking on what a good performance he had put in - not that verifications told you anything. Even in this made up online world of maybe make believe, no one is actually going to publish a poor review now, are they? And by the sounds of it, just about every male on the site was the best ride in town. "Don't let this one pass you by ladies." Oh, she'd heard it all before! She hoped in Andy's respect, that they were true recollections of his past encounters and that she wouldn't be disappointed come Thursday.

Andy was less keen to publicly display a face picture, as were many on the site. Lou herself was the same and tended to keep that revelation until they were serious about meeting, when the date and time were confirmed, etc. It was too risky, given her line of work and having a family, to give anyone and everyone access to what she looked like. There was no real way of knowing who was on the other side of the profile – fake or real. They could cause you

VANILLA EXTRACT

unnecessary embarrassment should they be that way inclined.

By becoming online friends, it meant that Andy could also see images that Lou kept from the public viewing. "You've got more tattoos than me and that's saying something," he told her. He openly admitted he was fascinated by them and wanted to know the story behind the ink, as well as wanting to run his tongue over every one of them. She teased him by saying she would tell him more 'in the flesh' when they met. She was equally curious to study his artwork too and imagined what a great mirror moment it would be if their bodies were naked and interlocked as they both watched. Lou had always found watching herself in the moment to be a great turn on and she was sure he would be great viewing too.

As Thursday drew closer, Lou began to feel a little nervous. She was going to a new venue with a total stranger. It was all rather alien. Andy put her mind to rest the night before when they had their first conversation on the phone about logistics. He sounded very mature, and again, very demonstrative. With a name like Impaler, she assumed he was of the dominant kink, but she found he was also very friendly and funny. "Don't think I'm expecting you to play with me just because you are my guest. I've been in this scene long enough to know that sometimes you just don't hit it off in that way. Do whatever you are comfortable with." This immediately made her feel better. Lou felt relieved

VANILLA EXTRACT

to find she was under no obligation. 'How very down to earth,' she thought.

While she was no swingers' club virgin, she did wonder how the night would turn out. (Lou attended a club a year before with a married couple and the wife's fuck buddy, but she had not yet ventured to this particular venue before.) Andy seemed to know the setting very well and spoke highly of it. By day the place was a naturist haven, with an outdoor swimming pool and cabins for naughty pleasures. By night, the club offered the same facilities but was more popular for those seeking an alternative 'club' evening out, with different themed events to meet the needs of the more sexually active and the depraved.

Reviews Lou had read of the club all echoed that the atmosphere was relaxed and you could do as little or as much as you wanted in full view of others or in private. It was certainly very popular on any particular night it seemed. The theme for this night was 'Easter Bunnies'. It was a privately run evening so she would get to sample what the club organisers' idea of a good night was, as well as familiarising herself with the facilities. Lou had the feeling it would be a lot of fun, and she was right.

Andy agreed to meet her outside a pub close to the club, as she had no idea where she was going. Lou pulled up next to him, and he motioned for her to follow him to the venue, which was less than five minutes away. The adrenalin was pumping through

VANILLA EXTRACT

her as they parked next to each other. She did love this feeling: part scared, part excited, and ready to have some fun. Gathering her bag and keys, he opened her car door for her. She knew she was right - what a gent!

"Good evening beautiful. You look stunning," he smiled as he greeted her. "Why thank you," she said. What a charmer too! He gestured for her to walk in front of him along the pathway to the house. Inside it was obvious he was well known to those working there, and he appeared to be well thought of too. He took Lou's coat and gave it to the receptionist. "Oh my god Lou, look at you," he said as he viewed her outfit. She was thrilled to bits with his compliment. She smiled and then bumped shoulders with him. It was their first contact and he felt firm! 'Mmmm,' she thought.

Walking into the house, Andy gave her a guided tour. It immediately put her at ease, just knowing where everything was. Looking and meeting some of the other guests, she did feel a little over-dressed, with her wine coloured short, fitted dress, stockings and six-inch heels. Many of the ladies there were already in their bunny outfits – not necessarily the stereotypical Playboy style, but basques and ears to fit the theme. Fortunately, underneath the dress, Lou had chosen a red corset that she felt amazing and sexy in. It was covered now until she was ready to reveal.

VANILLA EXTRACT

Andy introduced her to the organisers of the party. They both seemed very pleasant and welcoming, although one was walking around in his pants, with shoes and socks still on, which Lou thought was a little peculiar and not in the slightest bit sexy. They welcomed Lou to her first party with them and said they hoped to see her at many more in the future. Well, that would depend on how tonight went.

As both Andy and Lou were driving, they only had one alcoholic drink each during the evening, served by bare-chested butlers. All very decadent, she thought, but lovely too. These guys were super hot and well worthy of her ogling.

Andy couldn't take his eyes off her. "I'm so pleased you agreed to come tonight. I really didn't think you would." When she asked him why, he said that the pictures were so classy that he was surprised to have even received a reply to his message. Lou explained that whilst she was very down to earth, she did appreciate the finer side of artistic photographs. There were plenty of horror stories in pictures on the site. Lou preferred to leave something to the imagination, rather than show off what she had for breakfast between her legs online!

The conversation was flowing easily, and they both revealed that they found each other incredibly sexy. Andy was standing behind her as they looked on into the main room. The show was about to start, but they were more interested in each other. Lou didn't know what it was about having a man

VANILLA EXTRACT

standing directly behind her, breathing on her neck, groin pressing against her buttocks, but it drove her wild. She was in two minds whether to turn and eat his face right there and then, but he had said the show was worth taking a look, given it was her first time.

Instead, they moved into the room, where the butlers served chocolates, and then a performer began her routine. It was very glitzy and glamorous; a striptease with dancing, making sure all those sat on the sofas around the room were suitably worked up. She looked Brazilian and was absolutely gorgeous. But Lou and Andy were way too aroused already to watch. Their desire was too strong to stay here. "Shall we go check out a room?" he asked. She didn't need any time to make her decision. Off they marched excitedly to explore the rooms and each other.

Andy certainly knew his way around. He chose a room with a leather bed and told Lou to ignore the sign saying 'no shoes on the bed'. "I want you to keep yours on." She happily obliged. Her heels did make her legs look fantastic, and she felt more erotic leaving them on with her naughty outfit. He helped her out of her dress and hung it on the rather handy hooks to the side. "I knew you'd look amazing underneath that," he said and told her to lie on the bed. Following his instruction, she got on the bed and lay on her back. He immediately knelt down in front of her and began to lick between her legs, tenderly to start before moving very quickly to a more dominant lapping. He was masterful and knew exactly what he was doing. His tongue sent shivers through her and she wriggled in delight. Oh, he was good and she didn't want him to stop.

Before she knew it, he had her gushing all over the leather. Lou wasn't even sure where it had come from and why it had happened so quickly. It must have been the adrenalin and build up of excitement she'd been experiencing all night till this point. Whatever had caused it, Lou drenched most of the bed. "Oh my god lady, you sure can gush. I love it." She had no words. It was so intense, and her body was in shock. Lou was savouring every detail of this moment.

Andy's firm, fit body was above her next, and she admired the view. 'Mmmm, he is absolutely delicious,' she thought. She wanted him now to sample her oral skills. He grabbed some tissue from the side and dried the bed, so they could both lay down in more comfort. But that was not her intention. As he lay on the bed, she turned her focus to him.

Andy's cock was long and had great girth. It was the widest cock Lou had ever had in her mouth and initially, she didn't think she would fit it all in. With a bit of perseverance and lots of saliva, she managed to slide it in without gagging. So thick and so yummy, she couldn't help but give it her utmost attention. "At last," he shouted, "finally someone who knows what the hell they are doing." Lou took

VANILLA EXTRACT

that as a huge compliment particularly as he'd admitted being in the swinging scene for a number of years. Who knew exactly how many women had given him oral pleasure over that time? Lou was privileged to have been praised and continued making him gasp and moan with delight. She found his bulging penis to be quite a challenge, to be honest, but absolutely loved pleasuring him, especially when she saw and heard his appreciation.

It wasn't too long before neither of them could take it any longer. She so needed for him to be inside her. Reaching across to the bedside table, she grabbed a condom and handed it to him. He dutifully put it on, and she climbed on top of him, slowly sliding down. In fact, she had no choice but to lower herself very carefully. His member was gigantic and needed time to all go in! Once inside, she adjusted herself to manage its entirety. "Oh my god! Fuck!" she gasped. "You are enormous!"

Lou worked her way slowly into a rhythm. Andy was deep inside her and she could feel him at the top of her cervix. This was when she realised that his stage name 'the Impaler' was given for a very good reason. She couldn't ride too manically as she would likely hurt herself inside, so a gradual build up was required. "You ride me like a pro," he said. "It's fantastic." Lou thanked him, smiled and said, "You do mean a professional, right?" He laughed. Of course, he did.

VANILLA EXTRACT

"Now I need to fuck you hard," he stated as she smiled down at him. Lou felt another rush of passion with his words and exciting intentions. They broke apart as he lowered her on the bed. His massive cock was instantly inside her, and it couldn't get any higher. They had adopted the missionary position, but nothing was boring about this encounter. She was forced down on the bed, arms pinned in place above her head. She wasn't moving anywhere.

Andy was giving it his all and Lou felt every thrust inside her. It was so very deep and thick and seemed like it was colliding with her internal organs. Lou wasn't sure if she was going to be able to walk straight in the office tomorrow. "I want you to cum," she whispered to him. It was partly because she wasn't sure if she could take any more. Lou thought she might be sore if this carried on. "If you are sure," he stated. She nodded and before she knew it, the pace picked up. It was furious. It was rampant. It was fast and wild. Andy arched his back, took a sharp intake of breath and then froze. Hot thick cum filled the condom inside her as he stiffened up. "Oh my god," he shouted out then flinched as his body relaxed and very slowly lowered himself onto her.

Locked together, it felt very natural to be lying wrapped up in each other's limbs. They enjoyed the intimacy of the moment and held each other for some time before separating. It was then that they both laughed before it was time to clean themselves up. Andy carefully withdrew, making sure he left nothing inside Lou, then reached across and grabbed some tissues for her. Ever the gent, he was.

After reassembling their outfits, Andy said, "I suppose we should mingle with the other guests." They agreed to go party with the others. Lou didn't bother putting her dress back over the top of her underwear but instead held it in her hand. As they walked back to the main area, they were now bonded with a post-intimacy glow. There was more touching and caressing and way more smiling.

They were just in time to see the end of the next act, which neither of them was too fussed about, given the experience they had both shared. They watched it from afar, just outside the main room.

Feeling a lot more relaxed now with each other, their conversation continued and they found themselves talking about having sex with other people at the party. How would they let the other person know if they didn't want someone to join them? What if a man or woman wanting to play did not take their fancy? They decided that if anyone made unwanted approaches, similar to wrestlers, Andy and Lou would 'tap out.' It was a simple manoeuver, without words required, to let the other person know they were not comfortable to proceed.

Following this interlude, they chatted to a number of the other guests. There were some interesting characters, one of which was clearly a gentleman,

VANILLA EXTRACT

with short grey hair, a fully-grown beard, wearing a floor-length red ball gown. He took a shine to them both, particularly Lou, who made him feel at ease by saying she had a dress just like it at home. It wasn't necessarily true, but given he was standing out like a sore thumb, she wanted to make him feel comfortable. It transpired that he was Nigel, who had attended business meetings in London that day from Brighton and he was here to let his hair down.

Another couple were interested in playing with Andy and Lou as a foursome, but Lou wanted to keep Andy for herself. She had only just met him and didn't particularly want to share him. The thought seemed to turn him on when she explained this to Andy, and Lou found his hand stroking across her shoulders and tenderly down her spine as they stood there chatting. Lou enjoyed this affection and was happy to oblige when he suggested, "Let's go in the main room."

All around the outside of the room were double and triple sofas, with a large circular bed in the middle. Many of the seats were occupied with couples getting to know each other and others having full on sex. Andy guided her to a green leather Winchester settee at the far end. He was indicating for her to take a seat, but she suggested he sit down instead. Lou had an appointment between his legs once more and wanted to double check if she could get all of his manhood in her mouth again.

By chance, Nigel was sat on the sofa and was watching intently as she began. Andy wondered if

VANILLA EXTRACT

Lou was comfortable with this and with eye contact, she confirmed that she did not mind him watching. She happily knelt down between Andy's knees and began to devour her meal! He was bloody huge – FACT – and he felt incredible. He was rock solid and eager for her. She straddled him where he sat (after she'd indicated for him to put on a condom of course) and she lowered herself down onto him. Holy shit – SO good!

Their keen onlooker appeared impressed. It was clear that Nigel had been staring intently, more out of fascination it seemed. Lou had caught eye contact earlier and felt that Nigel was observing for inspiration, maybe to gain some tips for future use. He looked positively shocked as he watched Lou take all of that thick cock inside her.

Andy obviously had an eye on the circular bed and noticed that it was free. As she rode his penis deep, he stood up, picking Lou up in the process, and carried her to the middle of the room. Lou was totally surprised and wrapped her legs around him fully. She wasn't sure where he was taking her, as she travelled backwards in the air and still fully impaled, and finding it utterly thrilling. He threw her down onto the bed, for all to see, and with her legs up at his ears, he fucked her silly! Driving his penis deep inside her, she loved the performance, knowing she was quite literally the centre of attention!

VANILLA EXTRACT

Another man wanted to join in and started to stroke one of Lou's outstretched legs, as Andy took her. But Lou didn't want the distraction. She wanted to relish every hard pounding that Andy gave her. With a light right hand, she tapped his hip, indicating that she didn't want additional assistance or pleasure from this new stranger. Andy politely asked him to leave them to it, and the man respectfully accepted his fate, removing himself from their intimate show.

Andy enjoyed providing the entertainment as much as Lou did. Frequently looking around the room, he appeared to be accepting the attention and appreciation of the surrounding onlookers. Lou was enjoying the good fucking she was receiving in front of them too. Being watched was turning her on, and she gasped and moaned a little louder than she would normally have. The intensity of the sex, the watchful eyes and Andy's big, thick cock, made her cum all over him, and she made sure everyone knew it.

Lou's screams of delight had the desired effect on those around her. It seemed to bring the level of eroticism in the room to an all new high. Andy felt it too. Looking around and then down to Lou, he smiled at her knowingly. They had created this moment together. Her sparkling eyes and low sighs were enough to send him to the point of no return. He ground her even deeper and faster, and she could see he was about to explode. Harder, firmer, and there was the 'cum' face! The strength exuberated from his temples as the lion-like roar escaped his

VANILLA EXTRACT

mouth, except it was more of a groan than a roar, but it didn't really matter. The sheer delight was obvious, and another condom was filled!

More smiling ensued now. They were both quite pleased with their performances. After some readjustment of clothing and disposables, they retired to the kitchen. Feeling a little parched, the pair of them grabbed some water. Lou quite fancied a stronger drink, but she'd be driving home soon. 'Maybe another time?' she wondered. Andy certainly thought so. "I'm so glad you joined me tonight. I've had a blast," he told her. "I couldn't have asked for a better guest to join me. You've been amazing. Thank you," he continued. Lou was blown away. She'd had a fantastic night too and was thrilled she'd exceeded his expectations! She gave him a tender kiss on the cheek and a big hug and thanked him for inviting her.

Andy escorted Lou to collect her coat and then saw her safely to her car, as she received her Easter Bunny chocolate gift on the way. Another cuddle and kiss 'for the road' before she departed. It would be over an hour before she arrived home, but she did not mind in the slightest. She had the biggest smile on her face as she drove home in the darkness, reliving events from this adventurous evening. It had been a night of being outside of her comfort zone, and Lou felt a sense of achievement. She was buzzing all the way to the luxury of her lovely bed, where she slept like a log!

VANILLA EXTRACT

Andy would become one of Lou's special swinging friends, and she met up with him on a number of occasions after that Easter encounter. They had a mutual respect and relished time together, whether at clubs, parties or privately. Sadly the distance between them became impractical to maintain any longer-term form of relationship, but they kept in touch on Facebook and Whatsapp. They would regularly check in on each other and talk about the 'what if' scenarios. Lou accepted they would always think of each other very fondly - whether he was or wasn't impaling her.

VANILLA EXTRACT

Chapter 7 - Girl Friends

Lou' closest friend was, and continues to be, Millie. They met at primary school, although weren't particularly close then, and lost touch as they went to separate high schools and then on into their adult working lives. Some 18 years since they saw each other last, they found their paths crossing again, this time in adult education, as they had both enrolled into the same evening beginners' Spanish class. And so their friendship blossomed, as they discovered they had far more in common now than they ever had all those years ago.

At every next twist and turn of their lives, they were there for each other as friends, confidants, shoulders to cry on, babysitters and every other form of 'bestie' you could ask for. Now with seven children between them, one failed marriage and the other on the rocks, what else would they experience together? Well, as much as possible, was the answer to that.

Lou often thought about her gay brother's old friend Heather from years and years ago. She had grown up children, split with her husband (their father) and was now living with her girlfriend. Lou wondered how you could go from the usual vanilla set up to a completely different life, with a whole

VANILLA EXTRACT

new sexual persuasion? Was the straight life a lie or was it that Heather had fulfilled the conventional women's functionality and dreams? She'd had the fairytale romance, the beautiful wedding, given birth and nurtured three gorgeous kids. Now, what else was left to do? It seemed natural to Lou that Heather would explore 'the other side.'

At Millie's 40th birthday celebrations in Paris, after many a mojito, the ladies shared their views on porn and discovered that their favourite category to view was girl on girl, and maybe with a guy come join in later. There was not the usual hardcore pounding that you would find in male/female setups, well not from the start at least. The horny friends agreed that they enjoyed watching the passionate kissing and exploring, and could directly relate to it. After all, who knows a woman's body best? A female understands how delicately to caress a clitoris and when to build up the momentum to climax, where Lou found few men are patient enough in this area, rub furiously and then wonder why their partner has not had an orgasm.

Lou and Millie had become progressively turned on by their conversation but were a little nervous about doing anything else about it. They were getting increasingly drunk on the cocktail binge that had begun all too randomly, given the rain had started lashing down out there in those dark Paris streets. They decided to leave this discussion there, with some giggly knowing looks and promises of some further talk on this matter at another time,

VANILLA EXTRACT

probably when they were pissed again.

It was a few years before anything further actually happened. There were many occasions that female/female (FF) action was brought up, but usually after a few drinks, when the inhibitions were gone, and they would touch on this delicate subject once more. Increasingly it seemed inevitable that this would definitely happen between them, but they had a few practical concerns. Would it wreck their brilliant friendship? Would it change the way they were with each other? Would they regret it? It all felt a bit risky, but on the other hand, it was ever so exciting too.

Lou and Millie were the type of pals that wouldn't see each other for a while but would pick up the friendship immediately from where they left off. While it wasn't as frequent as they would like when they decided to make a night of it, they would make sure they went 'out, out'. This meant getting dressed up, wearing a little more make-up than usual, (not that either of them wore much anyway) and going out for a boogie. Pre-drinks would normally be at Millie's for convenience, and then both would get increasingly tipsy during the night on whatever cocktails came in jugs and could be consumed quickly.

Flirting and dancing were normally next in the evening course and they always had a really good laugh together. At some point in the night Millie would fall over, not necessarily from alcohol,

VANILLA EXTRACT

although mostly, other times from her weak ankles and inability to walk in heels. (Given Lou's work, she tended to be in heels most days, so she'd mastered them years ago.)

After a night at the local '80s bar and disco, Millie ended up kissing a man young enough to be her son. Meanwhile, Lou was lifted up and swung around like a rag doll by an equally young (and obviously very strong) man, after which the rather drunk twosome made their way back to Millie's house. It had been a really funny evening with lots of giggles and messing around.

Back at Millie's, did these party animals continue drinking? Of course they did, but they both knew their limits, and there was nothing better than a lovely cup of tea when they got in. Rock and roll ladies! Even during their drunken moments, they had their sensible heads on too, well mostly.

After their hot beverage, they proceeded to take their minimal make-up off, brushed their teeth and then settled into bed. As was usual, neither of them wore any clothes to bed, and they'd shared a bed in this way a number of times over the years. Tonight it was different. Tonight it was finally time for some exploring.

Maybe it was the alcohol, or maybe it was just long overdue, but both ladies were ready for this. They needed no words. It began easily and just like the porn movies they'd viewed separately so many

VANILLA EXTRACT

times, the kissing was electric. They were smiling incessantly, in between sliding their tongues in and around each other's mouth. This was way more natural and erotic than either of them had expected. It felt naughty, like some unwritten rule was being broken, but it also felt good. And both of these young ladies liked to feel good.

Caressing now began and their hands were all over each other, but it wasn't rushed or frantic. It was more sensual and very gentle. It was about the touching and feeling every sensation, as tingles on the skin and inside their bodies grew. Kissing deeply at the same time, their breathing became heavier and sighs escaped them both.

Lou began to make her way under the duvet to Millie's rather perky breasts. Lou thought they were less saggy than her own, which may have had something to do with Millie bottle-feeding her babies sooner than Lou had. Who knew? Who cared? What mattered now was how they felt and getting them in her mouth, of course, she laughed to herself. She took one in her hand and began to knead it before sliding her mouth around it. Flicking her nipple with her tongue, she could feel Millie's excitement building.

As she would with a male partner, Lou made her way down from the chest/breast area to her favourite place: between the legs. Millie had already begun to moan aloud. She was certainly enjoying this naughty attention and she was about to get a whole

VANILLA EXTRACT

lot more.

With both her hands, Lou parted her legs a little further and nestled her head in between them. Pulling her labia apart, Lou's tongue was soon focused on Millie's clit, tenderly touching it and kissing around it. Millie's moans stepped up a notch. She clearly loved it. Lou slowly slipped two fingers inside her as she continued to lick. "Oh god, oh god, oh god, that's so delicious." Millie began to grind against her and a rhythm formed. Lou applied a little more pressure with her tongue as she continued with her feast. Millie responded instantly and began grinding harder. With her left hand, Lou grabbed Millie's boob and began to play with it at the same time. It achieved the desired effect. Lou could feel Millie was about to cum. Lou increased everything she was doing - deeper in with her fingers, harder with her tongue, and now twisting her nipple. "Oh god, oh god, I'm cumming."

There was no holding back and no respite. Lou continued with her erratic motions until Millie extended her hand downwards and told her to stop. Millie twitched and jerked intermittently as her body enjoyed the explosion going on within her, but she could take no more! It was all getting too much!

Lou moved up the bed and held Millie. Wow! This was a whole new experience for them both. A few coy exchanges and some more giggles. "Wow. I didn't think that would be happening tonight!" Neither of them had expected it, to be fair. Millie

VANILLA EXTRACT

looked partly shocked but also very, very contented. She was grinning from ear to ear.

Once the mayhem happening inside her calmed down, Millie told Lou it was time for her have some fun. "I'll have what she's having," Lou laughed as she imitated the famous film line. Millie rolled herself around on the bed, so she was now kneeling. Squeezing Lou's breast lightly, she kissed her nipple before putting her mouth around it. Lou flinched immediately. She was super excited and every new feeling was more charged than the last. Millie slid a finger inside her. "My god, how wet are you? You're dripping." And Lou knew she was. There was no hiding it or controlling it for that matter, not that there was any need to. She was so turned on by this new experience.

Millie went further down and was now licking Lou's groin area. She didn't waste any time before devouring Lou's clit as her fingers played within. "I'm gonna have to mop up some of these juices, you dirty girl," and with that Millie proceeded to lap up her moistness. Lou was wriggling around like crazy now. She adored oral at the best of times, but this was even more exhilarating.

"I think it's time for Mr Harry," Millie suddenly told her. Lou had no idea what she was talking about. Millie got up and then pulled out a box from beneath the bed. So that's where she kept her toys! In fact, she had quite a collection! Lou knew she'd acquired a few over the years, but Millie really did need a bigger box! They were bursting out at the sides! "Naughty Millie," Lou said with a wink and a grin. This was fun!

Mr Harry really needed rebranding. It was more like Super Huge Harry - a much more appropriate description as far as Lou was concerned. Not only that but 'he' was black, which she hadn't expected. He could have been pink with gold stars - it was irrelevant. Lou was just wondering how on earth this enormous dildo was going to fit inside her?

Millie took Harry out and brought him to the bed. Kissing Lou tenderly she said, "I'd like to introduce you to my good friend, Harry. In fact, say hello to my little friend." But there was nothing little about him!

Slowly she began rubbing Harry on Lou's pelvic bone and up and down between her legs. It felt good to have a different texture on Lou's skin. Millie's gentle teasing motions were making her even more excited. Lou just wanted him now. She was desperate to find just how big he was inside her and whether she would be able to get him all in!

Millie ensured Harry was drenched in her juices before she slipped Harry's girthy tip inside. Checking Lou's reaction, she found it was just as she'd suspected. Lou could take it. Her vagina was practically enticing it in, and Millie found Harry happily delving deeper, as Lou's sighs began to increase. "Tell me he's not all in," Lou asked her.

VANILLA EXTRACT

"Afraid so, you bucket fanny!" Before Lou could retort, she found herself taking Harry again. Millie was getting into a rhythm, now plunging him in and removing again. "Ooooooh, so good, you biatch!"

Millie made her way down for a closer inspection. "I want to feel how Harry feels." Slowly removing him, she drew all the digits of her right hand in tight together and began to probe Lou's vagina with this newly found shape she had made. Gradually she went in deeper, but at a pace that she understood Lou could manage. Further inside they crept till finally, Millie's whole hand was inside. "How many fingers are in there?" Lou was curious after taking so much of Harry. "That would be all of them," Millie confessed. "Bloody hell," Lou cried. "What are you doing to me woman?"

With her hand inside, Millie decided she would add further intensity and began to flick Lou's clit with her tongue. "Oh Lordy, surely not?" Lou shouted. Could Lou bear any more of this? It seemed not. The oral was amazing with every other sensation she was experiencing. "Oh fuck! I don't believe it. I'm gonna cum!" With that Lou was in ecstasy. This orgasm was powerful! She came hard and strong, just how she liked it!

Looking down the bed once the tremors subsided, Lou was expecting some shared sentiments of euphoria but instead, and very typical of her best friend; a whole different scenario was happening. "What the fuck was that?" Millie had withdrawn her

VANILLA EXTRACT

hand, and it was dripping in Lou's creamy juices. In one motion Millie flicked it at Lou. Streams of fluid landed on her stomach. Lou laughed and pulled Millie onto her. "I gush, I squirt, I cum! What's a girl to do?"

After some cuddling, comparing and generally laughing, the ladies got themselves showered and back to bed. They had a long cuddle before they finally admitted exhaustion. They exchanged 'good nights,' and kissed each other on the lips, as was usual when sleeping in the same bed. They then simultaneously turned to face opposite sides of the bed. Millie and Lou knew they each slept best with no contact and having no one breathe over them. They'd learnt over the years that this had bugged them both about previous partners. Drifting off now was the most natural thing in the world, even more so after the exciting encounter they had just shared.

To these friends' utmost relief, this did not affect their relationship in any shape or form. While it was not a practice repeated (other than some kissing from time to time), they continued to be 'besties' who just so happened to know each other more intimately than ever before.

VANILLA EXTRACT

Chapter 8 - Close Call

It was a Saturday afternoon, on a sunny day in May, when Lou agreed to finally meet Lars. She couldn't quite remember why she hadn't met him before. Today he sounded flirty, with gorgeous new pictures online, and they both happened to have no plans. It was a perfect excuse to meet up and get to know one another after all this time.

Lars was renting an apartment close to where she grew up in East London. Lou was intrigued to visit her old stomping ground once more but even more excited to spend time with this rather gorgeous German young man. His plan was for her to park her car at his and they would take a walk over to Victoria Park. It was too glorious a day to spend inside, for now at least.

Lou arrived at around 1pm and Lars opened the door up before she had a chance to knock. He looked just like his pictures - tall, bald, athletic with very little body fat, if any. His tight blue shirt hugged his arms snuggly, and the fabric was clinging to his amazing chest. He was fresh and clean and she could smell his aftershave. He had made an effort for her, and she certainly appreciated it. Lou liked the look he was rocking, and she couldn't wait to be wrapped up in him.

VANILLA EXTRACT

They made their way across to the park. It was a short walk, and there she found it was filled with families enjoying the good weather. There were owners and their dogs, couples walking hand in hand and children on the swings. Lou remembered how lovely this place was – so open and free, yet right in the middle of London. Thank goodness it still looked the same as when she was a child and hadn't been consumed by new housing developments and the like.

Lars took her to one of the old East End pubs in the park, and they sat in the beer garden having some lunch and discovering more about each other. Despite messaging each other for some months online, they didn't know a great deal about each other at all.

After eating burgers al fresco, they took a stroll in the park. It was a great way to walk off the effects of a full stomach. At one point they decided to sit on a bench and take in the afternoon sunshine. Lars rested his head on her lap as he swung his feet to one side and lay down. As they chatted, Lou found herself stroking his face and massaging his scalp. He was very beautiful with sparkling green eyes that absorbed and threw back brightness. He was gorgeous.

The afternoon flew by and before they knew it, the temperature had dropped, so they made their way back to Lars'. All afternoon they had been speaking – about absolutely everything. There were no

VANILLA EXTRACT

awkward silences and Lou never at any point felt that she was searching for new topics to cover. It all flowed very naturally.

Lou found him fascinating. He worked in digital design, which was a completely different world to the finance one she was used to. His dialogue was unusual too. Whether this was the language, cultures or variety in their personalities, Lou found herself intrigued and at the same time was having lots of fun. Every conversation was a new one. She felt he was pushing her mental boundaries and she liked it.

Lars explained that he had recently started to explore cocktail making and was a dab hand with whisky-based ones. Whisky sours were his particular favourite right now, and Lou was keen to be his tester. Lars was true to his word. Lou found they were delicious! A few more of those and she knew exactly where this would end – in his bed!

Lou was right. It wasn't long before they kissed in his kitchen. It was tender. It was passionate. Lars swept her up and carried her to his bedroom. Lou wrapped her legs around his waist. She hadn't quite expected it. He was certainly strong, standing 6' 2" and broad-shouldered, with the physique of a swimmer, although he hadn't mentioned any aqua-related sporting activities as such. It was what Lou had surmised, which may have been wrong, but she didn't care right now. This was incredibly sexy, and she was an excited mass of energy and anticipation.

VANILLA EXTRACT

Moving into the bedroom, he knelt and placed her on the bed. Lou was mesmerized as he pulled down her trousers, pinned her legs down apart and began to give her oral pleasure. She could feel her juices building as he continued and it wasn't long before she was cumming all over his tongue. Bloody hell! He really knew what he was doing here.

Lars was now above her. Kissing her deeply, Lou felt his huge cock bulging against her stomach. He was a fantastic kisser. His kisses were slow and sensual, then becoming faster and more passionate. She wanted him inside her, and it wasn't long before she felt him sliding into her (safely of course). He was firm and strong, and he had control. Lou loved it.

"Push against me," Lars said. Lou complied. It was difficult at first as he held his full weight down on her and he was strong. It took all her strength to force herself upwards, while he fucked her hard. It was a huge turn on and a super work out at the same time. Lou was building up a sweat, but she was getting wet between her legs as well. This continued for some time – long enough for her to realise she needed to do more leg work in the gym!

Sensing her fatigue, Lars slowed down against her rhythm and withdrew. He had a pained expression on his face. "Ah, I think we have a problem," he said as he looked down and then at Lou. She wondered what was the matter and soon understood as she looked down at his naked cock. The condom was gone. It was buried deep inside her vagina and had come off during their intense sexual fusing. "Shall I?" Lou nodded, and Lars went in to retrieve it. His finger clasped around it and dragged the condom out. It was intact and soon discarded. 'Thank goodness,' she thought, although it wasn't ideal.

With a fresh condom put on, Lars continued. This time Lou's 'privileged access' rule was soon to be broken, as they both continued, so consumed in the moment. Granted, Lars didn't know what Lou considered acceptable sexual behaviour so early on in this encounter and what was and what was not allowed. They didn't discuss any of the do's and don'ts. But in the heat of passion, Lou made a conscious decision to continue, where in the past she would have told a partner to stop.

Lars had slipped his penis into her bottom as he towered above her. Normally this would have been an instant decline on Lou's part. Anal sex was something she considered a right and had to be earned. However, in this instance, as he gently inserted himself into her intimate and very delicate anus, Lou was surprised to find that it felt incredible. In fact, it heightened her sensitivity and was turning her on even more. Lars was also enjoying the sensation and began to move more quickly.

"Your arse is amazing Lou. It is so tight around my cock. It feels incredible," Lars said. 'Thank fuck for that,' she thought. Considering there was no additional lubricant used on this occasion, it was

VANILLA EXTRACT

sliding in and out (not exactly) painlessly, but quite effortlessly and it did feel good.

Lars built up the momentum and soon looked like he was going to cum. Lou looked up at him as his demeanour began to change. "I will cum soon Lou." She nodded at him in encouragement, and he did exactly that. The thrust inside her did hurt a little, but she knew it was the end, so put up with this finale pain as he came inside her. Lou was just pleased that he hadn't withdrawn his cock quickly, as she'd once experienced in the past when it had felt like her innards had been torn inside out. Of course, it hadn't, but the speed of a previous lover pulling out of her bum proved excruciating. Thankfully Lars was more considerate.

Lou noticed that Lars was also covered in perspiration as he lay down on top of her. They cuddled and exchanged more fluids now as their skin touched. They caressed each other gently as they spoke about the hot and steamy session they had just enjoyed. Comparing it to previous encounters, they both were pleased how the day had gone. So many other meetings with strangers had been less successful as they both recounted less positive stories.

Very slowly Lars withdrew from Lou. Again came a perplexed look on his face. 'What now?' she wondered. Looking down she noticed the error. On the end of his now almost flaccid member, was a gaping hole in the condom. "Oh shit!" Lou said as

VANILLA EXTRACT

she considered her arse being full of his unprotected semen. Her heart and her brain started to race. Was she safe? Was he safe? She'd already had his naked cock in her vagina when the condom came off, but no semen had been deposited then. Now the same and worse had happened in her bum. When were they both last tested for Sexually Transmitted Diseases (STDs)? It was time for some serious conversations.

Lars had been tested a few weeks back, and everything was negative. He had no reason to feel he had been unsafe with anyone else, so there were no issues from his side. Lou had also been tested negative around six weeks prior and also had no concerns since. For those reasons, and providing everyone was telling the truth, they decided not to let this spoil their day. What was the point? (Lou did decide however that she would get checked out again in a couple of weeks' time, just to be sure. Lars was probably thinking the same, for all she knew.)

In fact, they spent the rest of the night and the next morning in and out of each other! By the time Lou left, she was exhausted. Lars admitted she had worn him out too. ('Fist pump for Lou,' she thought to herself as she left and made her way home.)

Over the next few months, Lou and Lars only met twice more, due to him going off to Europe while his flat was being rented out for holiday lets. This meant he would be visiting Madrid, Barcelona and a number of other European cities. Lou was also due

VANILLA EXTRACT

to be holidaying in Ibiza for part of the time he was away, so their paths were unlikely to cross again until almost autumn.

Before Lou went off on her travels, she attended her STD clinic and was pleased to receive the all clear on the tests performed. She sent the information back to Lars, who was happily sunning himself in Spain. "That's great news," he said. "I still need to go and get checked out. I'll do it when I get back to the UK in September." Lou thought no more of it until he messaged her again upon his return.

Lou received a garbled message from Lars a few weeks later. "Lou, please ring me as soon as you can. It's important." Lou wasted no time in calling him. "Lou, I have bad news. I've been tested positive for HIV. Are you sure your results were negative? I've had to call everyone I've slept with." Lou was devastated for him. She could tell he was in despair and obviously hurting. "OK, honey. What's next for you?" she asked. Lars went on to explain how they were checking his blood counts so they could work out the best medication for him. He would know more in the next week or so.

Lou was in a state of shock. Despite her results being negative, there was the nagging doubt in her mind, following her call with Lars. She decided to get re-tested, just to be sure. Again, her results were all clear, and she let him know. By this time, Lars had been prescribed medication on a trial basis, to see how he responded and it was going really well.

VANILLA EXTRACT

Lars also established that he contracted the virus when he was first in Madrid. He had been with a transsexual, who at the time of their meeting had no idea they had just picked up HIV themselves. It was all very unfortunate.

Lou vouched to be even safer now going forward with her sexual health, even if the mishaps they had shared together were unintentional. Lou's new vice of sexual activity, albeit exciting and adrenalin-charged, was subject to such risk. She treated this experience as a sobering reminder that while this lifestyle could be seen as glamorous and to some more thrilling than 'vanilla', it was ever important to be careful. After all, it is exactly that - your life you are gambling with and all so easily you could be forced to change the style in which you live it with just one mishap.

VANILLA EXTRACT

Chapter 9 - Pearls of Wisdom

It was a chance encounter really, well in that it certainly wasn't planned and she wasn't looking for it. Lou had enough going on, with different meets lined up already. A mutual friend (Shantell) at work described a colleague of hers who had a very similar nature to Lou. Iain was apparently a highly sexual, attractive and horny little devil. He was an ex-British Jujitsu champion and still very keen on keeping himself in shape, with whatever type of challenge he set himself physically. He sounded perfect to Lou. Iain was also just coming out of a long-term relationship and was enjoying his newfound freedom. Shantell suggested perhaps they hook up and of course, Lou was never known to turn down such an opportunity for fun. She'd certainly go and take a look to see where this may lead.

Iain was apparently gob-smacked when Shantell showed him Lou's pictures. How had he missed her? They were in the same building after all, albeit two floors apart. Telephone numbers were passed on to each other very swiftly and so the adventure began. First, it was work's internal messaging system. Their initial messages were innocent enough, with an underlying knowing of exactly why they were both put in touch. Iain was full of compliments, which of course she adored and it was only a few days later that they met in person for lunch.

Despite being told, Lou completely forgot that he was Scottish, and this added to his charm on their first meeting. She waited in reception for him and was racking her brains trying to remember exactly what he looked like. She had only seen a very small picture, and it showed an amazing smile. Shantell said Iain was athletic, with a fit body and balding. (What was it with Lou and bald men? She was once told they were more virile and she had no reason or proof to doubt that theory.) Obviously she needed more than that to go on, but as it transpired, she had no need to worry. Iain was beaming when he came through the turnstiles, and the tight white shirt pronounced his amazing chest and muscly arms. Inside her head, she was already licking her lips.

They had already arranged to dine at The Canteen. It was just across the road from work and was tried and tested. It held plenty of tables for two and was not as noisy as some of the other establishments in the vicinity. Exiting work together they made their way over. The dialogue was the usual kind of awkward 'hello and get to know you,' to start with, but she soon felt very comfortable in his company.

At the table, the conversation flowed more easily, to the point where the waitress was sent back a number of times. They hadn't given the menus a second glance, as they began to discover more about each other, particularly about current relationship status

VANILLA EXTRACT

and interests. As anticipated, Iain was very much into his sporting activities and had participated in many mud challenges and other race events. Lou told him about her only ever mud event and how she would never, ever do another, unless maybe dressed in a bikini and wrestling a particular female friend of hers (or any other beautiful lady up for a laugh).

Food finally ordered, they continued to feast on the knowledge of each other. Iain had four children and was almost at the final point of being divorced. He had spent the last year or so as a free agent, and from what Shantell had told her, he had a very high sex drive, with quite a few conquests under his belt. It all sounded very similar to how she'd been spending her time of late - purely for research purposes, of course.

There were a number of occasions over lunch where Lou found him gazing across the table at her. This made her feel incredibly special. "You're staring," she said. "How can I not? You're gorgeous. You have amazing eyes and your smile is beautiful." 'Wow,' she thought. 'This guy is good. Not only does he look fantastic, but he has the gift of the gab too. What was the catch?'

It would have been obvious to anyone else at the restaurant that the chemistry between the two of them was explosive. If they had known each other a little better, weren't in the vicinity of work and had a few more hours to kill, Lou thought he would have

VANILLA EXTRACT

quite happily taken her over that very table there and then. She would probably have welcomed it too - such was the magnetism.

Lou didn't really taste the lunch. While the avocado eggs on sour bread with chilli was a usual delight; it didn't really touch the sides. She was more engrossed with learning more about him and wondering when exactly they could get naked together. She didn't mention this quite so blatantly, although it was definitely on her mind. Instead, Lou was coy, but giving just enough away to let him know how interested she was in spending a whole lot more time with him. To be honest, Iain could see it anyway. Her eyes were displaying the passion she was feeling inside. They were sparkling so much they were almost crystal-like, and he could see straight through to her desire. ('Darn it,' she thought, her eyes letting her secrets away again.)

Desserts during lunch hours were usually a treat for her. Normally she would not have the time or was 'trying to be good'. This time, however, he decided what was to be ordered, which she appreciated. Iain was ordering more than one sweet dish, and Lou was very welcome to have some with him. The two he chose were the best on the menu, she thought. Lou was happy to oblige in sharing them with him, even more so when she watched him make a start on the cheesecake. His mouth transfixed her. Lou couldn't help but watch every movement of his lips as he went in for each spooned refill. Now it was her turn to stare. Oh what he could do with that piece of oral

VANILLA EXTRACT

machinery, she could only imagine. Lou knew it was a matter of time before she found out first hand.

Sharing and swapping desserts, they spoke about mutual needs and wants. Lou explained that she categorically did not want a relationship (as she always told prospective conquests, always making it irrevocably clear from the start. From previous experience, it appeared that men didn't always seem to understand that, however, clearly she spelt it out). For Lou, it was all about fun and he looked pleased to hear that. No strings attached naughtiness together sounded perfect - to them both. She mentioned that she had found herself in 'mini' relationships over the past year or so, but around six or seven weeks was usually about the extent of them. By that time men had grown attached and wanted her all. She wasn't ready for that and was enjoying the freedom and irresponsibility way too much to be tied down, as such. Being tied up was an altogether different concept, however.

With no objections received, they continued on, turning the conversation to what they would now like to do with each other. Staring at each other's mouths and eyes, there was a hot passion between them, driving them closer. The animalistic emotion was desperate to be released. Sadly, they both had to go back to work, though it was unlikely that either of them would be able to concentrate that afternoon.

Back to reality, with heat emanating from her

VANILLA EXTRACT

knickers, she made her way back to her desk. It was hard to remove the childlike grin that had planted itself on her face. Greeting her was a message from him. "Thank you so much for a delicious lunch. You are beautiful. I can't wait to taste you." OMG! A shooting impulse went straight to Lou's already moist pussy. She couldn't wait for that either. Her mind was racing at the thought. When oh when could that be, she wondered? For the next two days, she would be working from home and then the weekend. Lou had to sort something out and fast! She needed him to be inside her as soon as possible.

Messaging moved from work systems to personal systems so they could speak more freely. It was obvious to them both exactly where this was going. The drive to explore each other was super-charged. Whatsapp took a beating as their messages flew in abundance. Neither of them particularly wanted to wait until Lou was next available after work, which was just under a week away. Until then she had her children to look after, so it was going to be difficult for any immediate skin on skin follow up. What a nightmare! This was proving difficult, but it was far too tempting to prolong.

While trying to plan their liaison, Lou considered her movements for the following week. On the Wednesday Lou was due out with some female work colleagues, celebrating a number of special events. One had got engaged, two had recent birthdays and she had just completed a huge work anniversary. As

VANILLA EXTRACT

she usually drove into the office, she was taking this opportunity to have a drink with the girls and stay in the area. When Lou mentioned that she hadn't booked a hotel yet, Iain immediately jumped into action. "Leave it with me," he said. "I'll book somewhere for us both." 'Sucker,' she thought but was pleased with this arrangement. It showed initiative if a little gullibility. She thanked him. "As long as you can amuse yourself till around 9pm." Of course, this was not an issue for him. Lou had now orchestrated the best of both worlds for her, including somewhere to stay. Men eh? So predictably lovely at times, and particularly when they 'think of things themselves!'

Back to her evening, now that next week was sorted. Sitting at home, she toyed with the idea of inviting him to her house sooner than their planned encounter. Wednesday did seem like an awfully long time to wait. Lou's kids would be away on Sunday night and the house would be empty. Initially, she had some reservations at this thought, as she'd only just met him and this was her private space. However, her instincts told her he was a good person and not likely to bring his axe with him. She sure hoped she had got that right. He was sexy as hell, and his messages were making her hornier still.

'Fuck it,' Lou thought. "Are you free Sunday night?" As luck would have it, he was. Immediately the excitement rose inside her. "Come over. Let's have some dinner and carry on where we left

VANILLA EXTRACT

off." He needed no persuasion. The date was set. Now she just had Thursday, Friday and Saturday to get through. Fortunately for her, she was having a 'tart week', and being childfree, her mind (and body) would be otherwise engaged for most of that period, but he didn't need to know that.

Given their cheeky, flirting messages over the next few days, it really didn't come as much of a surprise to her to learn that Iain had dabbled in the swinging scene himself over the years. When she mentioned going to a 'naughty' club in the next few weeks with a girlfriend of hers, he knew exactly what she was referring to. It transpired that he used to go with his wife in their younger days, before the responsibilities of children came along, whereas Lou had only indulged in this lifestyle relatively recently.

This gave him more appeal in her eyes. It meant he would understand her better and be able to relate more than someone from the 'vanilla' world of traditional relationships. Lou had lived the 'vanilla' lifestyle herself for most of her life and she wasn't knocking it. It was lovely if you found the right partner and were happy to explore other sexual scenarios and ways to express your inner beast just with each other, but she didn't want that now. Her post-marriage relationships failed with 'vanilla' guys when she realised they did not understand her need for sexual exploration and boundary-pushing. This added to her dilemma as to whether she could now fit into the 'normal' world in this way. She had experienced so much, but still the adrenalin rush of

VANILLA EXTRACT

new partners excited her. Lou wasn't ready for traditional right now. The question was - would traditional ever be ready for her again?

After a few somewhat exhausting few days, and an offer of a new sexual encounter during the day on Sunday, which she graciously declined, Lou was ready for him. She had wanted to be fresh and sex-free before they explored each other. The hours could not pass soon enough but finally, the meeting hour was upon them. She was nervous with excitement as he came to her front door. Iain was dressed in black jeans and a loose grey T-shirt. He smelt good, and again his arms looked divine, tightly tucked into his top. (She had shown his picture to her good friend Lucy, who commented on his gorgeous arms. He almost gained a new nickname of 'Arms', but the 'Pearls of Wisdom' won through.) Mmmm, they certainly looked good enough to chew on, and she was sure she would later.

It was a very warm evening. Lou had chosen to wear a short flowery dress with flat sandals. Her hair was straightened, and her make-up consisted of the usual bare minimum of mascara and a pale lip-gloss; the latter of which wouldn't be on long she doubted. She decided they would walk to the local pub. Iain surprised her by taking her hand in his as they set off. (She also wondered what her neighbours would think, but actually it was irrelevant. She didn't care to be honest.) It was a 20-minute walk through a tree-lined disused railway track, common to

VANILLA EXTRACT

amblers, cyclists, runners and horse riders. Somewhat overgrown, they joked about him protecting her from the stinging nettles.

It wasn't long before Iain stopped walking and pulled Lou close to him. He planted a delicate kiss on her lips, and she felt a rush of desire run through her. He was lovely and a gentleman. She kissed him back but slipped a cheeky tongue inside his mouth. He responded, and his tongue went straight in; like old friends, so comfortable in each other's company they tussled and danced in each other's mouth. "Mmmm, you kiss goooood," he said and she was beaming back at him. "So do you." They turned back and continued walking, but it wasn't long before they repeated the process. "At this rate, it will be dark by the time we arrive," she joked.

The walk took nearer to 40 minutes, with repeated stopping for kisses and the slow natural pace they adopted while finding out more about each other. Lou was intrigued to learn about his Cuban Pearls, which he informed her of over the past few days. Described as a piercing, they sounded more like an implant. Six metal beads inserted in the shaft of his penis; she'd never heard of them before. They were to provide more stimulation for the partner and not for himself. He had gone to this trouble to enhance things in the bedroom with his ex-wife, but sadly this was not enough to save their marriage. Whatever the reasoning, Lou considered this to be a new entry on her 'to do' list of firsts.

VANILLA EXTRACT

Spending time together outside of the confines of the work area was exciting. They both had a couple of beers but were not feeling any effect from the alcohol. Instead, they were more intoxicated with each other. Similar to the lunch date, they couldn't stop looking deep into each other's eyes and mouths. Typical that the food portions were enormous and it felt like forever that they spent inside the pub. But it was fun, interesting and intense all at the same time.

Iain paid and when they left, they kissed outside the pub. It was less tender this time. Despite the food, they were both incredibly ravenous for each other. They knew exactly what they wanted and needed. Tongues clashing this time and saliva flowed. Their eyes wide open, watching each other's expressions change as the wanting developed into severe lust. Lou could feel his heat as well as his hard-on and she wanted him. Regarding the other encounters she'd had this week, this was certainly the most passionate and her body had an immense desire for him. She could tell she was soaked!

Walking back seemed to take an eternity. Hands locked tight; they found themselves bumping into each other, kissing and touching, despite the urgency to get back to Lou's place pronto. When they finally arrived, she was so excited that she fumbled with her keys opening the front door, almost dropping them on the floor. How embarrassing and obvious how eager she was for him.

VANILLA EXTRACT

Finally, inside Iain held Lou close and proceeded to kiss her deeply once more. She couldn't help but gasp. It was exhilarating. Pulled in to him, she could feel the muscles in his arms and chest against her. They felt manly and strong. She loved his masculinity.

Iain's hand began to wander up her dress, where he felt inside her panties. There was no disguising her lust now. His index finger was soon inside her. He removed it and placed it slowly inside his mouth. "Oh, you taste so good. I want more." How could she resist?

They raced upstairs to Lou's bedroom where the fun really began, to levels she had only hoped for and anticipated he would achieve. She was not disappointed. He continued where he left off, fingers back inside her and this time passing the drenched finger from his mouth to hers. Reaching down he pulled her underwear down slowly and knelt on the soft bedroom carpet. He lifted up her dress and put his head between her legs. Ever so carefully his tongue was on her. It was delicate and just barely touching the surface of her eager pussy. Lou sighed blissfully. "Wow," escaped her lips. This was different, and it felt amazing. "You are gorgeous," he repeated.

Indicating they should move to the bed, Iain led her across and laid her down. She lifted the dress over her head, and he went straight to work on unfastening her bra, which he achieved with a single

VANILLA EXTRACT

hand. Feet on the floor still, her back was firmly planted, and he spread her legs to a more opportune position for him to devour her. "Well you didn't lie when you said you get wet," he said and began to tickle her with his tongue some more. It was divine. There was just enough connection to feel the sensation, with the anticipation of more pressure and probing. "Mmmm, that is so good," she moaned with delight. He continued now making his way all around her most sensitive area. Tasting her labia, licking either side of her clit, and then slipping his forceful tongue deep. "Oh boy," she let out without even realising. Another master of oral pleasure! What a lucky girl she was.

On their messaging of the past few days she had explained that while she loved to receive, she also liked to give, and she was eager to please him too, but now was not quite the time. He was as much a giver as she and he was enjoying providing her with as much pleasure down there as she could take - and for however long she wanted. What a result! She always took so bloody long to cum too, so this was a huge bonus.

Iain's skilful mouth was soon accompanied by his fingers, as he explored what made her sigh and moan the most. Lou loved every stroke. "I want to learn as much about your body as I can, so next time it's even better for you." "Be my guest," she stated as he continued to make her juices flow. Despite being on her own bed and not on a hotel one she could wreck, Lou didn't mind at this point just how much mess she was making. It was worth it. The sheets could soon be washed, and they would certainly need to be. She could feel the wet patch forming beneath her as the continual arousal showed itself in liquid form.

"You are so beautiful. I can feel your body contracting on my fingers as you cum all over them and you taste so good." He again licked his fingers, this time slowly so she could see the creamy texture coating them. "Now you're gonna cum some more." She felt the pressure quicken and deepen. Her body was trying to prolong the inevitable, but she was out of control. It was almost there and she could resist no more. "Oh boy, I'm so close," she screamed. It was barely three seconds later at most before the floodgates quite literally opened. "I'm cumming!" And Lou certainly did. It was everywhere. The bed was saturated, and she couldn't care less. She felt on top of the world!

Iain lay next to her as Lou's body absorbed every wave and tingle of the orgasm. It was only then that she noticed he had at some point removed his clothes. He was down to just his pants, and she had no idea when he'd taken off the rest. She had been so engrossed in the delights he was providing that she paid no attention to what else was going on around her.

As was usual at this point, following her orgasm, the laughter began. Lou's theory was that this was such a release of tension, which once emitted, she felt

VANILLA EXTRACT

light as a feather and so ultimately relieved, that it came out in a humorous form. A few laughs, sighs and hugs later and it was time for her to show Iain how good she was at providing him with the same euphoric feeling she had just experienced.

Full of smiles now Lou gestured for him to assume the position on the bed, preferably on a dry patch, as she was going to work. He removed his underwear first then slid up on the bed, so he was lying on the pillow instead of sideways, as she had done, and he began to relax. Lou was interested to see what these Cuban pearls were all about, but she would find out when she got down to meet 'him' and them in person. Right now she focused on kissing him deeply. Their mouths seemed to connect remarkably well. Hovering over him and leaning in for the kiss, her body caressed his. Her breasts lightly touching his torso and chest, this sensual approach was proving exciting for them both.

Moving down his body, she lingered on his nipples and chest. Lou was keen to see exactly what was going on with the pearls. However, before getting that far, what did surprise her was the amount of foliage down there in his nether regions. The majority of recent partners were trimmed or shaven, so it came as a bit of a shock to see that much pubic hair. It didn't put her off. It had just been a while since she'd seen so much and certainly made a change!

Licking around his manhood, Lou concentrated on

VANILLA EXTRACT

his thighs and stomach before she took her first inspection of the pearls. He had described them on their walk to the pub, and now she was seeing them for the first time. Lou held his shaft in her hand for a closer look. They resembled a blackberry to her, and she wondered if she'd be able to fit the girth in her mouth with the added width of the metal beads. For research purposes, she had to try. As it transpired, there was no need for concern. It was fine. She could fit them in, but she wondered if it hurt his skin when she pressed her lips against them. "No, they're fine thanks. They don't hurt. You carry on." And, of course, she did. She managed to put her mouth over them as she was sliding up and down his cock. He sighed with an appreciation of her oral delights, and she could tell either a) it had been a while, or b) he had never had it quite like this before. Either way and quite possibly both, she could tell he loved every lick, caress and nibble.

"I need to get inside you," Iain suddenly said. "I don't want to cum yet, but I do need to feel you around me." This was music to her ears and another spark to her vagina. He turned her on so much. From his bag, he grabbed a condom and put it on. Lou climbed on top very, very slowly, watching him intently as she slid him deeply into her wanton body. She could feel the Cuban pearls rub against her as he went in. They felt solid against her vaginal wall and gave her a different sensation altogether. It was like his cock was made of rock, and it was hard enough anyway without the additional metal. Sliding up and down riding him deep

VANILLA EXTRACT

provided additional friction with the pearls, and it felt great.

"You're amazing," came the sighs from the pillow. "You really know what you're doing; like you've done this before," he laughed. "Maybe once or twice," she responded. "Lay down," he said, and she complied readily. "I want to fuck you," Iain continued. Half in the wet patch, he pushed her legs wider with his as he knelt above her. She found this an instant turn on. Lou liked it when a man took control (not so much in a master/dominatrix way, just being forceful and manly). He kissed her mouth once more, staring straight into her bright blue eyes and he entered her again as slowly as she had descended before. An instant gasp escaped her as she took it all in.

"Mmmmm God damn," she laughed in some crazy American accent. She wasn't sure why but it just felt right at the time. And so the powerful fucking began. Every thrust of his hips forced him further inside her. This was incredible. Each probe caused her to take a sharp intake of breath. His speed of grinding increased, as was her gasping. It was deep, it was intense, and she loved every quiver he gave her body. She soon became aware though that her hands were going numb and her head was becoming light. (This was a sensation she had experienced with Snake Hips before in a few of their later encounters.) Lou didn't want him to stop. This was too good. Instead, she shook her hands around and then tried not to gasp with every jolt of his cock.

VANILLA EXTRACT

This seemed to do the trick. Less oxygen was passing through her and she could feel her circulation returning to normal.

This had obviously affected Iain too. He was getting sweaty with this most enjoyable cardio workout. Sweat was gathering on his bald scalp and was running down into his face. "I'm sorry, but I appear to be perspiring profusely," came his dulcet Scottish tones. She didn't mind this. It was good to slip and slide, but she was fearful it would drop into her eyes. She didn't want to close them as he penetrated her. Throughout this delicious encounter, they had been staring at each other continuously, so instead Lou reached up and licked the few drips that were soon to leave his face. Iain was somewhat surprised by this. Maybe this was a first for him, but given the exchanges of bodily fluids, it seemed quite natural for Lou.

More erratic and deep delving from above, she could not believe just how good he was. Fit too, what with all this exercise - he definitely had a high stamina level, which was fantastic! He was up there with her top performers! She wondered just how long this would go on for, not that she was complaining. Hell no! This was terrific.

"I want you to cum," she said. "I want to feel your body judder inside mine as you give me a piece of you." This was enough to send him over the edge. He began to growl as his motion quickened and became more erratic. Finally, it was too much. He

VANILLA EXTRACT

screamed out a prolonged, "FFFUUUCCCKKK!" This was followed shortly by "Fuck, fuck, fuck. Oh my god!" His body convulsed as he came hard. Frozen, he let it all out, and Lou held on for dear life.

Now it was Iain's turn to allow his body to recover. He quickly removed the condom, moving it out to the side so he could lie next to her. Their sweat-drenched bodies slipped perfectly into place, and they laid there laughing about the past two hours' activities. She wondered what on earth her neighbours would think about his outburst. It was certainly loud, and she was surprised they hadn't come knocking on the door to check everything was ok. They must have heard it!

Popping into the en-suite, Iain disposed of the 'debris' and used the loo. How relaxed they were now in each other's company and how very familiar! Lou did the same and they lay entwined on the bed recalling particular parts of the events so far. This only led to them becoming aroused once more. Lou was lying on his chest at the time, so it was a natural progression to go down on him once more. This time it was as if she had electrodes on her tongue. Every lick caused him to flinch. Iain's body was wriggling beneath her as she teased him some more and applied pressure to the top of his cock. "You were right," he laughed. "You said you'd make my back arch and you did it. Unfortunately, you appear to have killed him. I don't think I can again." She kissed him again, as usual with eyes

VANILLA EXTRACT

wide open, and laid back down next to him and they both snuggled up again. There was no rush.

Talking again they spoke about how sex gets even better with a regular partner. Over the course of time and meeting more frequently, you get to know what excites the other person. Other factors come into play too, like dressing up, spontaneous encounters, different places and the like. This conversation began to turn them on and it was soon very obvious that his cock was working just fine again.

Iain was soon above her once more, entering her slowly again as he stared into her soul. Round two was starting, and it proved just as exciting as the first, if not more so. They were at it like rabbits till 4am, despite it being a school night too. The alarm was set for 6am, which was a little earlier than required, but knowing full well their animalistic instincts would get the better of them once more, which of course they did. In fact, they were having sex for far longer than they should have and she certainly never made it into the office for her 8am start.

It was nearer to 9am that they both limped into work and wondered how on earth they would survive the day ahead. Their bodies were aching to the core but in the very best possible way. Sore leg muscles, arms, shoulders and more reminded them both throughout this longest day ever, of the wonderful night they had shared. The beaming smiles and naughty glints in their somewhat pink eyes would have told the true sensual story to their unsuspecting work colleagues.

Shantell had a lot to answer for. Good on her for bringing two like-minded horny buggers together. Both driven by carnal knowledge and a desire for incredible sex, it certainly wasn't the only encounter these two shared. In fact, it was around six or seven weeks, when they finally exhausted each other physically. Now they are very close friends who fondly look back at that exciting adventure, knowing they met their match in the bedroom, whilst never ruling out another episode of naughtiness.

VANILLA EXTRACT

Chapter 10 - Brandon, Anthony and Lou

Brandon had not been to a swingers club before, and he was keen to explore this phenomenon. Being a ballsy character, going into a club solo did not bother him, but what he wanted to avoid was being one of the sad single males who hung around the outskirts of the action, looking for a way in. That was no fun, surely? It reminded him of the old beauty competitions, where females would parade their goods, looking for recognition and appreciation. That was not for him.

Just as well then that Lou had a party night coming up at a club near Dartford and she would love him to be her guest. Having gone to a few different clubs herself, Lou had found that she felt most comfortable going in with someone or arranging to meet someone there, rather than showing up on her own and hoping to attract her 'type' of man. She felt less exposed (as it were) if she were accompanied than going in on her own.

As Brandon lived south of the River Thames, Lou picked him up at an overground station on the way. They were both supercharged and excited for the evening. Many messages had been exchanged throughout the day as the anticipation grew. He was concerned what to wear and she put his mind to

VANILLA EXTRACT

rest. Whatever it was, it wouldn't be on for long, she joked.

The theme for the evening was for older ladies to have their pick of younger men and so they fit the criteria, with Lou being over ten years his senior. They agreed that while they would go in together, they were then free agents to have their individual fun, as the mood took them. Brandon was clear that the evening would all be about Lou and whatever she wanted. 'Perfect,' Lou thought!

Going into the club, Brandon's nervousness subsided instantly. It transpired that he knew the event organiser and some of her friends who were helping out. He had been invited to a private party with them a few months before at the last minute and certainly came up with the goods! He was an instant win! This put his mind to rest, and the pressure was off. Lou had also met some of them before at previous nights out and really enjoyed their company. They had always been a lot of fun!

Anthony was sat by the door taking the entrance fees. He stood up as soon as he saw Brandon and the two of them had a hug. "Long time mate. How've you been?" It was quite a sweet exchange. They obviously had a lot of respect for each other. After some reminiscing, Brandon introduced Lou to Anthony, as they'd not met before. Anthony was hot; 'very young, but gorgeous looking,' Lou thought.

VANILLA EXTRACT

As they made their way inside, Brandon asked, "So what do you think of Anthony?" Lou gave her thoughts, and Brandon laughed. "I knew you'd like him. Do you want me to see if he's interested?" Lou was quite happy to go with the flow. After all, she was accompanied by a beautiful, fit, young hunk, as it was! She didn't need anything else plotted out for tonight, but if it naturally went that way, then why not?

The evening started with some games to make the party guests feel more at ease. This consisted of a quick-fire dating exchange as guys moved onto the next table after a given time. Lou wasn't interested in joining in and instead showed Brandon the facilities. Wandering hand in hand, Brandon saw there were four playrooms of various sizes. The smallest was more like a massage room, with barely enough room for the bed and not much more.

Next on the tour was the wet area, where two large jacuzzis were back to back, with occupants just in one at the moment, as the night was still quite early. Lockers were also here for storing clothes and belongings, as were the communal showers for pre and post fun cleansing. While they were there, they decided to lose some of their clothing and placed their outer layers in a locker.

Brandon was down to his pants and while Lou's white silky corset was beautifully fitted, she had omitted to put on the matching briefs and was walking around commando, with the hold-ups and

VANILLA EXTRACT

heels. She loved the libertine feeling and the attention this was bound to attract.

Brandon was keen to get into the empty jacuzzi, but from a practical viewpoint, Lou thought it would be highly unlikely that she would bother putting her play outfit back on again after being in there. Best to get some more effect out of her attire before the activities commenced! And that's not to mention the possibility of mascara running and soggy hair. It was not the look Lou was going for, well not at this stage of the evening at any rate. Way too much effort had gone into tonight's look to mess it up so soon!

Moving on, semi-clad, they came to a room with a large bed. The stable door was fully open, and the room was empty. At the end was a chaise longue, which could be useful later, they agreed. They were now feeling considerably more fruity as they continued their tour.

Next door was set up like a mini cinema, with sofas pointing to a TV screen showing pornography. There was just one occupant, being an older gentleman dressed only in a towel, who was gently stroking his cock as he viewed the film.

Departing the room, they threw each other a mischievous look. Despite agreeing upfront that they would probably play separately, it seemed a waste not to use the facilities now, especially considering how fired up they both felt.

VANILLA EXTRACT

Brandon led Lou back to the room with the vacant bed and chaise longue. They began kissing frantically. His spade-like tongue was back in action and lashing at hers as he threw her onto the bed. God how she loved when he took control! Getting rather self-involved they didn't notice the man enter the room and close the door behind him. Instead, they continued battling tongues and starting to feel each other's passion growing.

Out of the corner of her eye, Lou noticed the stranger sit down. She nudged Brandon and looked over at their unwanted roommate. Brandon immediately questioned him. "What's happening, fella? We don't mind you watching but leave the door open. This isn't a private viewing." The stranger apologised and opened the door up. Whether this was a wise move or not, Lou and Brandon would decide later.

Lou left the corset on as Brandon moved down her body. Her arms naturally moved above her head as she enjoyed the licking that commenced. He was the master after all in this area. Before she knew it, another naked body appeared kneeling on the bed, respectfully back from her head, but the cock being massaged in view was bound to get closer if she didn't make her thoughts clear. The same was said for another body that appeared to her left. Lou made eye contact with the first man and indicated that she did not want him to join in with them. He accepted his fate and the other man nodded in agreement.

VANILLA EXTRACT

Lou was getting seriously worked up enjoying Brandon's oral skills but also knowing other people were getting off by watching them. Her sighs grew in volume and her wriggling around was possibly a little exaggerated. She loved this shared pleasure, and it only further accelerated when she noticed the room was filling up. They were drawing quite a crowd.

"Brandon, come lay on the bed." Lou swapped positions with him and began to devour him in front of the onlookers. They were enjoying it as much as Lou was and the wanking seemed to intensify throughout the room. Some did try to get closer to her, brushed against her as they rubbed themselves, but Brandon was her focus. "I need to be inside you," he said. "Get yourself back down here." Lou instantly complied, much to the approval of her voyeurs. There were sighs and moans of "yes," as she took her position back on the bed.

Brandon slipped on a condom, knelt in front of her and held her legs out splayed for all to see. With her heels at his shoulder level, he entered her slowly then began to furiously fuck her hard. It was exhilarating for them both. "Holy shit!" Lou screamed, probably louder than she would normally have. She loved the thrill of their reaction. It was mesmerising and turning her on even more.

Feeling Brandon pumping her deeper and deeper each time, she looked around and saw the room was

VANILLA EXTRACT

completely filled. In fact, people were being turned away. "There's no room," she heard someone say. 'Bloody hell,' she thought, lapping up the atmosphere.

Lou could sense, however, that all of this excitement wasn't being appreciated by both parties. It was all getting too intense for Brandon. Lou could feel his cock softening. She got up from lying and was sat straddling him. She whispered in his ear, "Are you ok hon., or is this a bit much?" He told her he was losing concentration with all the bravado and she could sympathise. It was nuts! "Let's find a different room," she suggested, and Brandon looked relieved.

"Sorry guys, but we're gonna take this somewhere a little more private now," Lou told the crowd. There were a few sighs and "aaaaah" comments. The man who had remained closest to Lou throughout said, "Thank you so much for a brilliant show. Just wished you'd sucked me off at the same time," with a wink. He wasn't being obscene. He was being witty, and they laughed. He shook Brandon's hand and said "Good job!" 'How funny,' Lou thought. You can go from putting on a live sex show in a room full of masturbating men to then chatting very normally with them straight after.

Having disposed of the protection and rubbish, Brandon collected his pants and socks from the floor. They decided to get a drink before venturing into the massage table room. Their performance had left them sweaty and thirsty, and that room had

VANILLA EXTRACT

become incredibly hot. The next room of choice was too small to let anyone else in - excellent! It did have a stable door too, so you could allow people to watch, or not, without entering.

Lou made Brandon lay on the bed first. She wanted to suck him back to full strength, and it didn't take long at all. By this point, having been built up before but not cumming, he was desperate to let it all out, after a bloody good fucking first. Fully erect, he indicated for Lou to swap positions, as before, as he put on a fresh condom. With legs akimbo once more, he proceeded to pound her hard. Lou's legs touched the walls on either side, and even with the top section of the stable door open, men were looking in and caressing what they could reach – mainly being Lou's left leg, that was up in the air.

"Oi oi," came a shout from outside. It was Anthony. Surreally, with his cock still inside her, Brandon and Anthony struck up a conversation about what they'd been up to since they last saw each other. Lou thought this was hilarious and decided to play with her clitoris while they continued. With his penis locked in, it was adding to the stimulation she was providing. Hearing her gasps, the men turned and realised she was close to orgasm. They decided to leave Brandon to it and chat later. Wise choice given it wasn't long before Lou came all over his cock! 'Mmmm,' Lou thought. 'I needed that!'

Once driven and now with a taste for it, they decided it was time to move on to somewhere a little more

VANILLA EXTRACT

comfortable. Onwards to one of the other rooms where some group play had ensued. Brandon recognised Casey and Jenny on the bed. Jenny was happily being slammed hard from behind as she was licking another lady's pussy next to her. There were gasps and groans aplenty from both women as they were becoming more and more turned on. The other female was sucking on another man's ball sack before he plunged his cock inside her mouth. She could unquestionably deep throat while receiving oral. Meanwhile, another couple who didn't seem as comfortable placed next to this entangle, were just finishing off. This certainly looked like a room to join.

Lou and Brandon walked towards the chaise longue. Lou told him to sit down, and she immediately pushed him back and kissed him deeply to get him in the mood. Once he was relaxed, she stepped back and knelt down. She took his cock in her mouth and began to make it grow for her. Just as she was having success, someone else came into the room and sat next to Brandon. It was Anthony, and he seemed to still have his clothes on.

The boyish banter began once more and Lou maintained eye contact with them both. Brandon was indicating that Anthony should get involved in their fun, checking with Lou first that she was happy with it. Lou was very excited and thought it was a perfect idea. Anthony took his trousers off and put them to one side. Down to his pants, he was about to sit down, when Lou shook a finger at him to

VANILLA EXTRACT

indicate 'no'. With her mouth full, she couldn't verbalise it, but Anthony understood what she meant. Only once he had removed them was he allowed to join them.

Lou continued with Brandon, as Anthony was obviously getting very aroused. She saw his cock was humungous, at least 10", maybe more, and thick too. The girth was wide. As Anthony stroked this beast gently, Lou moved across to her left, where he sat. At the same time, she heard Brandon say, "She's fucking amazing mate. I don't know what it is she does with her tongue, but just you fucking wait." Lou then laughed out loud. "I am here you know!"

Spending time now on Anthony's cock, Lou was keen to impress. She worked her usual magic, running her tongue up and down his shaft slowly before she plunged it all inside her mouth and made sure she looked up from time to time. Brandon and Anthony were comparing notes, and it was all sounding very positive. Anthony was trying to talk in between gasps and Lou was quietly finding it quite funny, particularly when she applied some pressure with her tongue. "Fuck! Shit! What the fuck?" It was working! Lou continued for a short time after and then moved back across to Brandon.

Instantly Brandon's head went back where he laid and he enjoyed Lou's naughty mouth. Anthony continued to caress his penis, eagerly awaiting her lips once more. Lou gave Brandon enough attention to make him feel special, but given they had already had fun, and would be spending the rest of the night together, she returned her focus upon Anthony.

After some more of her delights, Anthony said, "How about I take you while you suck Brandon off?" Now there was an offer she wasn't going to refuse. Anthony put a condom on and stood behind her. Very tenderly, he slipped his massive cock into her. Lou was thankful. He was a bit of a beast after all! OMG, he felt good inside her. That coupled with having another cock in her mouth was mind-blowing.

Lou couldn't quite believe this was actually happening. It was something she had wanted to do for a long time, but always thought it was something she would have to research, plan and orchestrate. Instead, here she was, being spit-roasted, by two gorgeous, fit and hung young men. Delicious! Lou didn't think she could have improved on this scenario if she'd planned it herself!

"Let's swap," Brandon said, as he was putting a condom on. Anthony withdrew as Lou turned 180 degrees. Anthony's cock tasted of rubber, but it didn't matter. Lou was prepared to put up with this as it meant she could continue this thrilling moment. Now Brandon was giving it to her as she sucked Anthony. Could this night get any better?

After some pounding and sucking, a space became available on the bed, as a couple were putting their

VANILLA EXTRACT

clothes on and leaving the room. The happy threesome decided to move onto the bed instead to continue. Casey and Jenny were still enacting their debauchery openly as Lou lay down. Brandon continued to pump her, at the edge of the bed, standing just at the right height. Anthony was to her right, and conveniently at mouth level with his huge weapon! Lou carried on where she left off.

Anthony didn't appear to want to fuck Lou again. He was having a fantastic time with his cock being devoured in such a way. Lou found his balls were being offered to her face, so she nuzzled into them and began to nibble all around. It was too much for him. "Oh God Lou, I'm sorry, but I'm gonna cum! Where do you want it?" "All over my tits please," she instructed. Casey squealed from the bed, "Anthony was brought up well. You're SO polite!" They all laughed as Anthony shot his load all over Lou's breasts as Brandon continued to thrust her hard.

With hot, cum all over her chest, Anthony looked a little bit embarrassed. "I'm sorry I came so quick. I was just so excited." Lou responded, "Don't be daft. Thank you, both for my first MMF!" (Her male, male and female threesome cherry was now popped.) With that, she offered up her hand to Anthony for a high five, which he reciprocated. "I'll get some tissue," Anthony said. "Oh, he's housetrained as well. Nice one Anthony!" Casey couldn't help comment it seemed, but it was funny, and they all laughed once more.

VANILLA EXTRACT

Once Anthony had wiped up the deposit he left, he told Lou that Brandon had his number and he should give it to her. He would like to see her again, but next time for it to be on their own, if Lou was willing, which she most definitely was. She'd give him a call in a few days. He then gathered up his clothes and left the room, at which point, Brandon pushed Lou further onto the bed. Now was their time!

Without any other interruptions, they could relax and resume their marathon fuck fest! Just as they got into their flow, there was a knock on the door. It was the doorman telling them it was time to get ready to leave. The club was about to close! Oh, what a shame – just as they were getting into it as well! Sadly they had to cease their interaction and make their way to the locker area, where they put their clothes back on. Lou's legs were shaking, making it difficult for her to balance as she dressed. 'All the signs of a most enjoyable evening indeed,' Lou thought.

Brandon was also very pleased how the night had gone. He was positively perky given it was now 3am as they drove off to his house. What they both realised, as they made their way to London, was that they were both famished! All the exercise they had all partaken in had left them rather hungry. There was nothing to it – they needed to find a 24-hour fast food establishment. At 3.45am they found themselves in a drive-through McDonalds woofing down quarter pounders like there had been a

VANILLA EXTRACT

famine! It felt like it was the best meal they had ever had and it lasted around three minutes maximum.

Suitably nourished, they continued their journey to Brandon's, where, despite all the night's activities, they were still both horny, and managed to get another round in before they finally passed out. Now would be their time for all out and uninhibited explosions (Brandon's first of the night), and that's just what they had followed by heavy, albeit brief sleep. Lou and Brandon were shattered, but it was well worth it!

VANILLA EXTRACT

Chapter 11 – School Disco

The 'school disco' theme was just an excuse to wear very little and look sexy, knowing full well the outfit wouldn't be staying on for very long. It was Lou's first swingers' house party and she was very excited. Someone from the site had recommended this particular venue and she was really pleased that her newly found female friend, Lucy, was up for coming along too. It would be the first time they had met in person.

When Lou arrived at the hotel, she was even happier to find that Lucy had arranged for a mutual friend, Andy (The Impaler), to be joining them, and he just so happened to be hung like a donkey! Both ladies had the pleasure of him separately prior to tonight and before they had met. He never failed to fulfil them both – with or without his signature cock ring. Lucy had also brought two other delectable associates of hers: one beautiful female, Sabrina, aged 22 and a fit, 'cut' male called Ben, of 25 years; both delicious. Oh, tonight was going to be fun! The more, the merrier!

They arranged for Lucy to have her outfit ready and waiting for Lou, bearing in mind Lou had just disembarked a plane from Majorca, jumped in the shower at home, applied make-up very swiftly and

VANILLA EXTRACT

shot round the M25 all within two hours. Lucy was already wearing her own twin version of the same costume. She had dispensed with the short-sleeved white shirt that was supposed to be worn underneath the incredibly short tunic and instead exposed her matching bra and knickers set. By chance, Lou had chosen almost identical underwear, in black and pink instead of black and purple, and the outfit was almost complete. A quick tartan tie addition, thick black over-knee hold-ups and high heels adorned, and they were ready to go!

Arriving at the venue, they met with sliding entry gates. The house was far bigger than Lou had anticipated and she was grateful for the guided tour, which made her feel more comfortable. Downstairs consisted of a large open kitchen, which was set up with mixers and glasses at the ready. Next was the dining room, with chairs all around the outside and a large table full of various snacks for those already hungry or looking to nourish an appetite they would build up later.

The lounge area and potential further dining area was set aside for a dance floor, with dance pole at the ready, and DJ in residence getting the crowd in the mood. He was controlling both the music and the projector, which was showing erotic pictures from previous house parties held at the venue. There were two bathrooms to choose from, which she was sure would come in handy later.

VANILLA EXTRACT

Outside the large patio area was starting to fill up with more couples and single females, all dressed in their various school ensembles. The atmosphere was very friendly and as newbies, they were made to feel very welcome. Armed, as directed, with sparkling rose wine and some cans of gin and tonic, they were shown where they could be stored. It didn't feel like the sort of party where you had to watch your drink in case it got stolen, and this proved true.

Across to the right was a huge indoor pool and after poking her head in to have a look, Lou retreated quite quickly. This was not due to any embarrassment having seen a few couples sexually entwined, but because she found the heat was unbearable. She doubted she would be going in for a dip later – not in there at least.

After a drink on the patio and mingling with some of the other guests, the small horny group felt it was time now to go upstairs and have a look around; maybe even to start playing, although apart from the pool area, no one else seemed to be doing so just yet. The men were very keen!

Upstairs they found two further bathrooms, a 'dark room' and two massive bedrooms. A loft ladder extended up into a dungeon, fully kitted out with a love swing, ropes, restraints and other sexual paraphernalia – 'interesting', she thought. They headed into the bedroom that had an adjoining balcony overlooking the garden. The flow of air

VANILLA EXTRACT

made it more pleasant as it was beginning to heat up in there, and not just the room itself.

All five of them were getting rather excited and very horny with the prospect of getting to know each other more intimately and playing as a group. The outer garments soon fell to the floor and party time commenced. Lucy was entertaining her bisexual side already and was kissing Sabrina while pushing two fingers inside her vagina repeatedly. Behind Lucy, Andy exposed his huge penis momentarily before lunging it inside her forcefully. Lucy gasped with delight as she took him all in and continued to pleasure Sabrina as he fucked her hard.

This left Ben and Lou, who were kissing aggressively, as they lay down on the king-size bed next to where their friends played together. She ignored his revelations that he preferred older women, as they apparently knew exactly what they wanted – even women older than her! She didn't quite know how to take this remark. Lou thought it was supposed to be a compliment of sorts, but it felt like it had the makings of an unintentional insult if she was sensitive about her age – which Lou wasn't. To be honest, right now she just wanted his cock, so she turned a blind eye to his youthful ignorance and thoughtlessness.

What Ben lacked in prowess and charm, he made up for in physique, which was amazing. He stood 6' 4" and had not an ounce of fat on him. She marvelled at his six-pack and ran her tongue across the contour

VANILLA EXTRACT

of each one of them. It was like an old-fashioned washing board and she enjoyed every crevice.

For some reason, Ben seemed to think he would be the one starting the activities, but she was ravenous and didn't particularly want to hear anything else he had to think or say. She turned her attention straight to his large erection, which was already dribbling in anticipation. "I've never been able to cum from a blow job," he said. Now whether it was his naivety or her vast experience, but her immediate thought was, 'oh not that old one again.' If she had a pound for every time she heard it? It was a line guys used when they wanted you to give them a good sucking as if they had to trick a woman into doing it. Some men just didn't understand that there are women out there who derive enjoyment themselves from giving oral pleasure. They really do revel in it. Lou told him, "Well I'm not going to promise you will cum from this blow job either, so just relax and enjoy what I'm going to do to you," she said and chuckled to herself inside. What a total novice he was!

Ben was not disappointed, even though he didn't cum. She had his back arching within moments and his hands grasping at the bed sheets as she turned on her charms! "You should teach younger women how to do that," he called out at one point. Again – was this a backhanded compliment? "Maybe offer lessons?" Oh, he was full of them. She couldn't really see herself putting that one on her CV; 'Blowjob mentor to younger, less experienced ladies.'

VANILLA EXTRACT

No, she couldn't quite see that helping her career somehow, well not unless she decided to veer away from her corporate one in the finance world!

There were condoms all around the room, so she reached across and gave it to him to put on. Once protected, she climbed aboard his huge penis. After the manic night she had so far in getting from another country to this point, Lou was ready to lower herself down on him. 'Mmmm,' she thought, 'just what I needed.' She continued to ride him deeply for some time, and he felt good inside her. Her thighs were getting a good work out, as were her innards. However, it was all feeling a bit mechanical and whilst the sex was ok, he wasn't stimulating her mind and she was beginning to get bored. It did feel a bit like fucking for the sake of it.

"Let's get some air," she said, as she dismounted and waited for him to adjust himself. Their friends were now out on the balcony and Lucy was kneeling down to suck Andy's throbbing cock. Sabrina had gushed all over the bedroom floor by Lucy's clever handy work and was 'gathering her thoughts' while watching the others. She looked very subdued as Ben moved out onto the balcony and across to her, caressing her shoulder as he went in for the kiss.

Meanwhile, Lou imagined the thrill Andy would feel at having his two favourite ladies both on him at the same time. (Privately before tonight, Lucy and Lou had agreed he would be their first FFM [female, female and male threesome] together, as he had

VANILLA EXTRACT

definitely earned the right from his previous performances). She knelt down next to Lucy and joined her in tasting his delights. They passed his cock between their mouths, kissing each other in between, as he looked down upon them in pure glee. A beaming smile was planted across his face, and he looked like the cat that had got the cream.

To add to the pleasure, Lucy reached back and found Ben's naked body close to her. Tweaking his nipple, she turned and began to play with his cock as he kissed Sabrina. Andy pulled Lou up to standing position and kissed her neck tenderly before turning her around, so she was looking over the balcony at the party guests below. Putting on a fresh condom, he slipped his pulsating cock into her and fucked her from behind, much to the mutual appreciation from those looking up. The volume of Lou's gasps and moans suddenly increased as the pounding continued.

Lou was having the time of her life. There were no rules. She could be herself and do what she wanted to do. Not only that, but everyone around her totally accepted her. In fact, she felt so comfortable in her skin that her attire for the rest of the party comprised of a Velcro necktie, over knee stockings, heels, and nothing else. Every other part of her fancy dress outfit had been cast aside. Lou didn't feel the need to bother putting them back on after her encounter with Andy and the show they had put on for those keen voyeurs below them.

VANILLA EXTRACT

Walking around the party, leaving nothing to the imagination, Lou revelled in the attention she was receiving from the other guests who had not yet de-robed. She loved how very friendly everyone was, and she stopped at various points en-route around the house, just chatting with others and enjoying meeting new people. Everyone was very complimentary of her attire, her tattoos and her figure, which fed her ego tremendously. She lapped it up as she walked around and entertained her social butterfly trait.

There was a particular man Lou kept crossing paths with on her numerous mingling circuits. He was a rather dashing gentleman, older than her usual type of late (which currently meant anything above 30 really). He had a cheeky glint in his eye, which she liked. There was definitely a mutual attraction, as they struck up a growing conversation each time of passing.

His physique told Lou he was a rugby man, doubtful that he played now, but he certainly must have done in his time. Grey hair, slicked back, broad shoulders, fit body; he had it all going on. What let him down were the poor fitting Calvin Klein pants he was wearing. Hardly school disco, but that wasn't the issue. They just didn't do him any favours. They were baggy when that style was usually worn best when they were tight and showed off a man's shape. Lou was just pleased that he was barefooted. The socks and shoes look did nothing for her when the

VANILLA EXTRACT

rest of the body was on show, as she had witnessed elsewhere before.

"Pants!" she shouted and pointed down to them as they crossed paths again in the kitchen. He smiled and stopped to talk with her. "Hello gorgeous," he said. "I've not seen you at these parties before. Is it your first time?" And so the connection was cemented. The conversation flowed smoothly and she liked the way he was looking at her. There was lust in his eyes, and she imagined him taking control of her. Lou explained who she had come to the party with and confirmed that she wasn't 'with' any of them in a relationship kind of way. He had also come alone, though knew many of the guests from previous events.

Just as they were getting to know more about each other, Sabrina came up to Lou and asked if she had seen Lucy. She seemed a bit concerned, so Lou offered to help find her. To Pants, as he was then to be known as, she said she hoped to catch up with him later. This turned out to be a mistake she made there and then. Lou should have stayed, continued talking with him and seen what would have transpired between them. Lucy was bound to be ok and Sabrina was maybe panicking unnecessarily. Lou had no doubt too that if she remained with Pants, that it soon would have turned very sexy.

Instead, she went on the search for Lucy. It was the right thing to do, even if Lou's loins were telling her differently. As expected, Lucy was very quickly

VANILLA EXTRACT

found being pounded by a young, very good-looking man, in the front bedroom. He was standing at the edge of the bed, fucking her from behind as she licked out his girlfriend who was laying legs straddled apart on the mattress in front of her. She was not in any harm but instead was having a great time. "I'm so sorry Lou. I couldn't find her earlier, and I was getting worried," Sabrina said. It wasn't a problem. Always best to look out for your friends. Especially in unfamiliar circumstances, with people you don't know, however comfortable you may feel.

Sabrina and Lou moved back into the other bedroom where they found Andy and Ben having lots of fun with some other ladies. A couple were watching them from the side of the room and started talking to Lou. "Oh good. You've come back. We were watching you earlier and wondered if you wanted to join us?" They were not an unattractive couple. Caught up in the moment and before she knew it, Lou was going down on the man while he kissed his wife/girlfriend where they were leaning on the wall. He was really enjoying it when she noticed out of the corner of her eye that Pants had come into the room. He looked like he had been searching for her and immediately she wished she had stayed with him downstairs.

Lou made her excuses with the couple she had just begun to pleasure. "I'm sorry guys, but I'm needed elsewhere," she told them. "Well hurry back," the man said to her, but she knew she would not be returning to them. And so her epic hunt began. Lou

VANILLA EXTRACT

performed numerous loops of the property in search of Pants. It seemed he had disappeared. A couple he had been speaking with earlier confirmed he was still around, but she just could not find him. She wondered if he was looking for her too, but they were continuously missing each other.

Andy and her other friends were ready to leave in a while, but Lou was very much still up for partying, particularly as she wanted to find Pants and exchange telephone numbers at the very least. She confirmed with Andy that she would be ready in about half an hour and he was fine with that. He had his sexual fill tonight, so was pretty much content to go with the flow.

The last room she tried was one she had only popped her head into before. It was the 'dark room', and it was packed full to the brim with debauchery! Her thoughts on dark rooms were quite strong, and she tended to avoid them in general. This was mainly because of her fear of a) catching any sexually transmitted diseases, particularly if you can't see if a condom is being adorned and b) not quite being able to see who was pleasuring you (and she had very high standards of those she wanted on her and inside her).

Lou was carrying a huge glass of vodka and lemonade but knew she didn't particularly want, especially knowing that her friends were ready to depart soon. As she went into the room, the first thing she noticed was how humid and hot it was,

VANILLA EXTRACT

and not just the temperature. It was naturally pitch black, and she could barely make out a mass of bodies all tangled and giving each other sexual gratification. She could not see who was who and whether Pants was even in the room. "Does anyone want this drink?" she asked. "It's vodka and lemonade." "Lou, is that you?" A muffled voice came from the sprawling bundle of bodies. It was Pants, and he immediately broke apart from the woman who was sucking his cock, to come over and speak with her.

Lou felt bad about breaking this happy harmony up, but Pants confirmed it was fine. Lou also noticed that as soon as Pants came to speak with her, his previous partner was soon receiving attention from those around her. She was not in the slightest bit bothered about him getting up. "I've been looking all over for you," she said. "But I thought you were busy," he explained. He was right. It had looked to him that she was would be spending time with that couple, and hence he moved on and found someone else to have fun with. But the couple were not what she desired, and she told him so.

After explaining to Pants that Lou would have to be leaving soon, he asked if he could at least show her what he was capable of. "We really don't have enough time," she said, but he convinced her to sample his tongue work, which immediately commenced where they stood. First, he kissed her tenderly, holding her jawline and exploring her mouth. As she began to enjoy his taste, she felt

VANILLA EXTRACT

someone kneel in front of her and begin to lick her clit. It was a massive turn on. The man on his knees was picking up the pace, and she felt fingers inside her. In and out, in time with his kissing, she became very moist very quickly. Only when Pants motioned to lie on the bed did she realise that not only had she been receiving oral skills from the man beneath her, but the digits entering her did not belong to the same man. Another guy on the bed behind her had been finger-fucking her while she was being kissed and licked. She just loved the naughtiness of that, even if he wasn't really her type!

Lying on the bed, he moved his way down her body and continued with his oral pleasuring. He was certainly skilled in this department, and she soon was enjoying every lap of his tongue. Lou's past fears of the dark room were soon expelled as she drifted off into his passionate devouring. Moments later she was brought back down to earth as light suddenly filled the room. She saw Andy open the door and enter the room. He was looking for her, and she motioned that she would be with him very soon. It really was time to leave and she couldn't really let her friends down, despite this rather erotic situation. Pants saw too and asked if she really had to go which, of course, she did. They left the dark room and went downstairs, exchanging deliciously knowing looks as well as their phone numbers. Their time had been cut short, but they both knew this was just the beginning.

VANILLA EXTRACT

Luckily for Andy, it seemed Pants had warmed her up, and she was ready for action back at the hotel. Luckily for Lou, Andy's stamina and sex drive was high enough to give her another round before sleep beckoned them both, and he always had plenty to give! While Lou didn't experience the wild crescendo orgasm she so desired usually, the night had lots of highlights and pleasures she would smile about long afterwards. 'Wow - what a party! What a night!' she thought as she dozed off contently with a big smile on her face.

VANILLA EXTRACT

Chapter 12 - False Marketing

Having chatted online for a few weeks, Lou thought it was time she met Mark. He came across as funny, articulate and a caring sort. They shared intimate stories of previous sexual encounters as they got to know each other. They even compared not so pleasant experiences that life throws at you, ultimately about how cancer had touched both their lives. Her father had passed a few years ago and Mark's mother was currently fighting it. Lou felt there was a bond forming on a personal basis as well as potentially physical, and it was growing daily, the more they messaged.

They agreed to meet at Hammersmith underground station, which was about half way for them both. Six o'clock was the time to convene on the shopping mall concourse, and Mark gave clear instructions on the best place to wait, whoever arrived first. Lou wasn't that familiar with the site. She hadn't been there for years and it was bound to have changed from when she used to attend music concerts at the Odeon there in her teenage years.

At 5.45pm Lou departed the train and made her way out to the shopping area. It was a chilly night and not the best time ideally to meet. Commuters were bustling their way through to get home as quickly as

VANILLA EXTRACT

possible. She found herself being moaned about as she found her bearings and worked out where she was going. Unfortunately, being in the opposite direction to most, it had already pissed off a few of miserable commuters.

Passing a few pop-up make-up stands on the way, she thought she'd hit those on the way back, given they had a large selection of nail polishes, for which she was a complete sucker!

Heading to the allotted meeting place and fighting against the human traffic, Lou continuously scanned everyone around her to see if she could spot Mark. At the exit, she continued looking while dodging some determined office workers who had no interest in her plight. There was no sign of him, but then she was a few minutes early. Perusing the location, she decided to move back into the warm. There was no point waiting out there in the cold.

As Lou went back inside, she noticed a guy who had had been walking in the tide of people going the other way earlier. Could this be Mark? It was always a bit of a gamble as to whether they would look like their pictures. She'd never seen Mark with glasses on before, but then she could see a resemblance to this man. He looked across at her but with no expression. If it was Mark, then he didn't appear to be sure if she were his meet either.

At this point, Lou's phone rang. It was her eldest daughter ringing for a chat. Lou decided to walk

VANILLA EXTRACT

back to a bench she had spotted earlier, and there she sat to continue her conversation. Lou had no intention of walking back to the exit to see if Mark was there, not when it was so cold.

Lou decided it was Mark she spied earlier, which was confirmed when he walked back again, in the same direction as Lou this time. They made eye contact again, but Lou looked away, diverting her gaze. There was no way she was going ahead with this meet.

Mark was dressed in a shabby tracksuit (and we are not talking shabby chic here). It resembled one of those 1980's shell suit outfits, made of poor quality material, and it was covered in paint. He had white sports socks showing up to mid-way on his shins and the tracksuit trousers were tucked into them. It looked awful. The trainers were old and on their last legs, so to speak, again covered in paint. He looked a mess and in the split second of realising it was Mark, she decided there and then that she wasn't prepared to spend any time with someone who hadn't made an effort for her. This meeting had been in the diary for a few weeks, so there was no excuse to turn up looking like that.

Following her telephone conversation, Lou got up, walked back to the make-up stand and purchased two new nail polishes. There was no point in making this journey a complete waste of time. Jumping back on the train, she headed back towards her work. A colleague was leaving and having a

VANILLA EXTRACT

celebration at one of the bars there, so Lou went along for a couple of soft drinks before heading home.

Lou felt a sense of sadness but relief too when she logged on later. There was a ranting message from Mark stating how he thought she was a better person than that and would not have wasted his time being a 'no show.' Now it was time for Lou to confess. "Oh, I was there Mark. I was there early and stayed for about half an hour all in all. Was that you in the white tracksuit?" His tone changed completely as the excuses came pouring out. He had to come straight from work. He was totally busy. He wouldn't normally dress like that when meeting someone, and so it continued. Mark guessed he'd blown his chances. He assumed she wouldn't want to meet up again. He was right.

It may have been harsh, Lou thought, but she was annoyed. When you make yourself look presentable and travel halfway across London to meet someone you may just have a connection with, the least you can expect is for them to do the same! She was also a busy person, who had also been at work all day, but she still managed to look good for him.

Lou moved swiftly on and felt no remorse what so ever. Lou had standards, and unfortunately for him, Mark fell below them. She was not prepared to compromise. Well, why should she? ...Next!

VANILLA EXTRACT

Chapter 13 - Pablo

It was just another normal Friday, or not quite in Lou's case. As if standing stark bollock naked, drinking beer at a kiosk on the beach with fellow Brits, Germans, Belgian and Norwegians, wasn't out of the ordinary enough, her day was going to get even crazier.

Lou had decided to take herself to Gran Canaria for a few days on her own. It was somewhat of a personal challenge she set herself: to travel alone and chill out away from the normal hustle and bustle of home life. So far Lou had done quite well. There were a few funny things that had happened already during this adventure, the first of which was realising, when she checked into her hotel, that she was quite possibly the only single female there, and very likely the only straight person in the vicinity. Lou remembered when looking for resorts that there were many adult-only and 'heterosexual-friendly' ones to choose from. Lou amused herself. She knew now she must have chosen the latter!

Another clue was the unexpected additional essential in the hotel bathroom. Along with the usual toiletries, you become used to seeing, like shower gel, shampoo and conditioner, was the packet of two condoms! They had thought of everything! But

VANILLA EXTRACT

what she loved about being surrounded by fit, gorgeous gay men was that she wasn't going to be hassled in any way. The last thing they would want to do was to come anywhere near her, especially when there was so much adorable testosterone to choose from!

Back at the beach, Lou was speaking with an older British couple that frequented the island. As with many she met, they came to Gran Canaria time and time again and loved the naturist lifestyle. They were staying in a completely naked resort and said they would never go back to being on a beach with swimming costumes on. "Why would you want to sit around in soggy Speedos?" Chris had asked her. His point was well made.

The German couple that took Lou under her wing a few nights before were also standing there drinking their beer and Sprites (or shandy as Lou knew the beverage) and speaking with others from their homeland. The first time they had gone to the kiosk, they thought the usual rule of covering up out of respect applied, but they soon dispensed with the outer garments for fear of looking odd! On the other hand, Lou had clocked the etiquette from the start and soon settled into the natural bathing and equally natural drinking. When a small gathering joined them, they became a naked human shield from the wind!

A few beers in, the sun was blistering above and amusing banter flowing between them. It was a

VANILLA EXTRACT

great way to be spending her last full day of her mini break. It amused her just how easy it had been to fit in here, and she was sure that the other people on the beach thought she was a regular too. It all felt very natural (literally), and 'normal', if ever there was such a thing. They had no idea that this was her own personal experiment to see how she would cope, and that she was doing just fine!

When guys came up to get drinks or food, it was obvious that they were checking Lou out and she found she was doing this too – seeing what was on offer and whether she wanted to pursue it. She always had a strong sense of this - whether eye contact, body language, or being more blatantly up front.

Lou's peripheral vision was on high alert today (as most days), and she soon spotted this rather beautiful man as he laid his towel out a few metres away. He was only young, perhaps around 30, and his body was perfect. It was lean, toned and muscly but not over the top and no evidence of steroids. His hair was short and his beard was trimmed, and he looked like he would soon be on the prowl. She was right.

The Adonis made his way all around the entire kiosk and ended his journey standing by her side. His English wasn't very good, and neither was the appalling chat up line about what the time was. But none of this mattered a single iota. Striking as he was, what was more up front was the ten-inch semi-

VANILLA EXTRACT

hard penis that he was waving around freely without even trying! Just about everyone standing around was looking at it in awe. It was a beast! Lou tried not to be focusing on it as she spoke with him, but it was proving difficult! Adding to the somewhat awkwardness, were the friends she had made at the kiosk, who were currently giving her the thumbs up signs behind his back! Lou did her utmost not to laugh out loud.

Lou was finding it a little embarrassing, as he was coming onto her and trying to kiss her with all the others watching. She indicated that they should move away from the group. They made their way to his towel on the beach to continue their broken English/pigeon Spanish conversation. Thank goodness for Google Translate! It was proving incredibly useful as they typed into his telephone and had their thoughts instantly translated.

Glancing up the kiosk, Lou could tell the others were all talking about the size of his cock, as they kept looking over. It was rather magnificent and seemed to grow each time she looked down. Whilst she sat with him she noticed he had pre-cum rolling down it and pointed it out to him. He soon wiped it away but was not embarrassed in the slightest.

"I am Pablo. I live the feet. I have foot fetish. I live suck the toes. I live the sex. You?" 'Ok,' Lou thought. 'I get the gist of what you mean here, but if he goes near my toes, I'll probably kick him.' This was not even to push him off but a natural reflex.

VANILLA EXTRACT

Her feet were very ticklish, and it would be dangerous physically to go anywhere near them!

Lou was not sure how to proceed. Should she take him back to the hotel? She was naturally suspicious and had to think sensibly here, even though her desire for him was growing. Did she really want him knowing where she was staying or near her possessions? She would think about it. Well, that had been her plan – to ponder a bit further, until she spoke with Pedro, the sunbed man (who rented out beds to sunbathe on) and had a funny conversation with him first. He said, "You love sex. You want sex. So why wait to the hotel? Have sex now and then have some more sex back at the hotel." Well, that was true! Why wait when you could have double? This resulted in Lou agreeing to go into the sand dunes with Pablo, and finding a quiet spot for naughtiness. Just as well she had put those free condoms in her beach bag. You just never do know when the need was bound to arise, as it were!

Pablo directed her to the homosexual area of the dunes, as it was less likely to attract single men who wanted to watch and masturbate at the same time. Lou compared them to Meerkats, popping their heads up out of nowhere. They could be so annoying as they got closer and closer, which she'd found out earlier in the week, and a little intimidating too. Pablo's choice was a good one. It was deserted, funnily enough, for most of the time.

They found a dip in the sand and put their towels

VANILLA EXTRACT

down. Pablo reached over as they stood and kissed her again. It was quite sloppy, but he was forgiven. He'd be forgiven anything looking like that! He was fully erect, and it was absolutely enormous. Lou thought he would want to get straight down to it, but instead, he wanted to give her oral pleasure while looking at her feet. Who was she to argue? Even with his tongue lapping her pussy, she was finding it a little difficult to relax. She would have preferred to be pounded there and then, but she went with the flow!

Knowing she would not reach orgasm in these circumstances, Lou took control. Motioning for him to stop, she turned her attention to him. Somehow Pablo had managed not to coat his cock in sand while he was down on her. The towels helped, despite the wind blowing sand around them. Lou had wondered if it would be like an ice cream cone sprinkled with hundreds and thousands by the time it came anywhere near her! It did look good enough to eat, and it would be rude not to!

Lou knelt down in front of him and took his penis in her left hand. It took very little for it to find itself in her mouth, but she could not fit all the length inside. Pablo was grunting quite loudly with every suck. "I live it. Oh si, oh si, oh si!" And on it continued until he said, "I want fuck you, ok?" 'How very polite,' Lou thought! He reached into his bag and produced his own condom. 'Resourceful too,' Lou contemplated. It was obvious this was a regular occurrence for Pablo, and she

VANILLA EXTRACT

could understand why with that weapon between his legs!

Ensuring he had put it on, she then turned around on all fours. Doggy was the way, particularly if he was too big for her. It always made men come quicker, not that she wanted to get this over and done with, but a good ploy in case the monster cock hurt. He entered her slowly and remarkably, to her delight, she found herself being very happily fucked by him. It wasn't painful, as she'd anticipated, but very satisfying. His moans were rather loud, but she soon switched off to that.

'Turn to back,' he suggested, and she lay down on her back. He wanted to look at her face, but possibly more her feet. He guided her legs up into the air, wiped the sand off her right foot and kissed her toes. Lou was a bit squeamish with her feet, given how sensitive they were, but she managed to keep it together and not boot him in the face. But what a sight for Lou to be looking up to! His chiselled face, shimmering green eyes and beautiful body above her was divine, not to mention the fully loaded machine that was moving inside her.

"I live the foot," Pablo said as he began to suck her big toe. It was too much for her. She squealed as she wriggled her foot away. Pablo apologised. Lou showed him she did not really enjoy the attention her foot was receiving, so Pablo concentrated on his end goal. More powerful thrusts and, "Si, si, si, si, si," followed by a chaotic removal from Lou's pussy,

VANILLA EXTRACT

as he took off the condom, let out an almighty growl and spilt his load all over her. It had some velocity! It went everywhere, reminding her of a previous fruity lover of days gone by. A huge dollop shot straight across her right temple, across her hair, and the rest was deposited over her stomach and his shoulder. Like a scene from 'Something About Mary,' Lou wondered how that was going to look going back to the kiosk group! Her hair would probably be standing up by itself!

Pablo had kitchen roll in his bag, for such occasions, and offered it to her. He was quite sweet actually. She cleaned herself up as best she could and was now feeling content, even without an exploding orgasm. He asked her to lie on his back in the sand, which she did. It felt lovely. His skin was smooth and warm from the activities, as the sun beat down on her naked body. Lou was relieved that her body was still intact despite their encounter. She had a huge smile on her face and the bonus of still being able to walk. Result!

Hand in hand they made their way back to the kiosk, having no idea really how long they had been in the dunes. Most of the kiosk gatherers were having their final drinks before packing up for the day. "Oh, we wondered if we were going to see you again," Chris greeted her, smiling. "And you're not hobbling," his wife added! Both had a knowing look in their eyes. She said, "We thought you were the luckiest lady on the beach today, and every woman, and probably every man too, was

VANILLA EXTRACT

jealous." Lou laughed. "I did my duty for inter English/Spanish relations and mutual appreciation," she retorted.

Lou bid them farewell as this would be the last time she saw them, although they all agreed, her included, that she'd probably be back and see them later in the year! Pablo continued to hold her hand as they walked the shoreline to the taxi rank. It was all very romantic until they started talking about their ages. He seemed genuinely shocked when she revealed her age, but not as surprised as she was when he said he was 25! 'Oh dear,' she thought. 'I've broken my own age rule again, although unknowingly.' It was a little too late now to worry that this conquest was nearer to her eldest daughter's age than her own age. Hey ho!

Pablo may as well come back to her room after all, given what they already got up to at the beach. Lou warned him (via Google Translate) that she had to pack her case as she was flying home the next day. This gave her an excuse to extract him from her hotel room when she needed to.

Back at the hotel, there was a knock on her door. Lou immediately became suspicious. What if Pablo had arranged to meet friends here and she was about to be robbed, or much worse? Cautiously she opened the door as Pablo stood to her right. It was 'Mr. Fit', the resident masseur and gym instructor. 'Phew,' she thought. As usual, he was smiling and looking amazingly hot. His tight t-shirt was

VANILLA EXTRACT

accentuating his broad chest. "Did you still want the massage? I am here all night. Just let me know." Lou felt bad now. She didn't like letting people down or misleading them. She had previously promised him she would have a massage before she returned to England. "I have a visitor at the moment but how about in one hour?" Lou suggested. That would work perfectly, she thought and would be her reason for Pablo to leave, particularly as he was getting very cosy sitting in her room. He was happily and quite beautifully singing in Spanish to music from his phone – all totally in the nude. And while this was delightful on the eye, she was keen for him to leave soon.

Getting her beach bag emptied and case contents packed for her morning flight, Lou summoned Pablo to the shower. He happily obliged. It was a chance to get the sand out of all those nooks and crannies ahead of her massage and it meant that she could apply bubbles all over his divine body as the shower washed them away.

There would be no fucking as it was in the shower and without protection. Instead, she knelt down underneath the newly reawakened beast and began to pleasure him, with her hand first and then her tongue. The groaning began, and more rounds of "Si" escaped him. He clearly loved the shower action, and it took no time at all for him to cum! This time it washed straight away, rather than landing all over her – a relief all round!

VANILLA EXTRACT

Hair cleaned, body sparkling and then moisturised, Lou chose simple clothing for the massage - G-string and bikini top, covered by shorts and a vest. Pablo and Lou headed down to reception together. Telephone numbers were exchanged, for messaging (minimal as that was likely to be), big hugs all around, and he left the hotel with a smile. What a very nice afternoon Lou had enjoyed with him. Time now to prepare for pampering, followed by a night out on the town before leaving this beautiful island.

VANILLA EXTRACT

Chapter 14 - Mr Fit

While sunning herself at the gay hotel, Lou was approached by the resident masseur, who explained the services he offered and their associated prices. From that point on, every day she saw him he would ask when he could perform a neck and back massage, or an all over body. Both sounded very tempting, but she kept putting him off, not because she didn't want this indulgence, but more that she was so busy. Since arriving, Lou had been having a great time with the various people she met. She was out late every night but didn't want to miss out on any sunshine either. Her trip was short enough as it was and she wanted to go home with a decent all over tan.

Finally, they agreed Lou would have a massage on the day before she was returning to England - Friday. Given he was gay, she felt comfortable to joke with him and teased, "Only if there's a happy ending!" He laughed and said she was a very naughty girl. Lou thought it was a shame he wasn't interested because he was also the gym and yoga instructor, and naturally fit as fuck, was Mr Fit.

After her eventful day at the beach, Lou was ready to relax. Making her way across the reception, Lou entered the spa area, where Mr Fit was waiting for

VANILLA EXTRACT

her to administer some serious pampering. What a lovely way to be spoilt before her final night out

He welcomed her in and closed the door behind her. Soothing music filled the room, and various candles were lit, adding to the calming ambience. There were two beds available, for couples' massaging, but they were going to use the one closest to the door. "Please take off your clothes," Mr Fit instructed her. Lou did a double take. Did he mean all of her clothes or should she leave her underwear on? "What – all of them?" she enquired. "Yes – all of them - naked," Mr Fit explained. She was a little shocked by this. 'Well that is a first,' Lou thought. Upon looking around the room, however, she noticed all the pictures of de-robed men enjoying their treatments. It did appear that being naked was the norm. When in Rome... or in this case Gran Canaria...!

Lou piled her clothes in the corner, albeit a very small pile. Feeling a little self-conscious, she made her way to the bed, climbed aboard, laid on her front and placed her head in the right position. This felt great already and quite liberating. She never knew where her arms should go on these things. Should they be bent up and left either side of her head, palms up by the sides of her bottom, or dangling over the edges? Mr Fit said they should go wherever felt comfortable. She went for the palms up version and prepared to drift off to a heavenly place.

VANILLA EXTRACT

Mr Fit began to work his magic once he had smothered oil over Lou's back. His touch was firm, as she'd expected with that muscular body, and the circular motions over her shoulder blades was pure bliss. He asked her about her day and whether she had been to the beach. Lou said she had spent most of the day there and had a lovely time. Having come up to her room to ask her about her appointment earlier, he had seen Pablo inside. "Your visitor is gone?' Lou was a little surprised by his question, but she didn't feel embarrassed. She confirmed he had left just before coming to the spa, which Mr Fit would have worked out anyway.

Mr Fit moved to the other side of the bed, but as he did so, Lou felt his groin area rub against her arm. 'That's a bit odd,' she thought, as she distinctly felt his penis stroke her through his shorts. 'Surely not,' she wondered. He was gay after all. Lou tried to put naughty thoughts out of her mind. Maybe it had just been an accident or a coincidence? But Lou didn't believe in coincidences.

Next, he began to work on her left leg. His fingers and thumbs delicately caressed the back of her thigh, from left to right and right to left. To Lou's surprise, she found she was starting to get a bit of a twinge in her lady regions. He repeated the motion, going up and down her thigh now as well as across, and she felt a positive flutter. 'Ooh this is feeling good,' she was thinking, but for all the wrong reasons. His fingers were definitely rising and moving inside her thigh more and more with each stroke. In fact, it

VANILLA EXTRACT

wasn't long before she did get a stroke, right between her legs, albeit made to appear unintentional.

Lou could feel herself getting more and more turned on. Was this really happening? Mr Fit was speaking, but it was hard for her to concentrate, to be honest. "What sort of massage you like?" Ah, it was a fair question. "I like all types of massage, but I'm not particularly fond of the Swedish massage," Lou explained. He looked puzzled. "I'm sorry, but my English is bad. What you say?" Lou lifted her torso to show him a demonstration of this type, and he understood. "Ah ok," he said. "Do you like sensual massage?" Pa-doing! If she had a cock, it would now be pointing to the ceiling! Well, that was unexpected. Lou was so sure he wasn't straight, but apparently women were not off his menu at all. A little bit dazzled she responded, "Oh, ok, sure, why not?" How surreal could this day be?

Mr Fit repeated the motions at the top of her thighs and brushed her labia again. Her body was now reduced to a tingly mess, and the anticipation of what was coming next escalated her excitement to all new levels. Lou thought she was ready for anything but hadn't quite expected to find his tongue now so expertly placed between her legs, caressing her rather wet pussy. Licking intently, Lou had no idea how he got there but OMG it felt fantastic.

"Turn over," he said and she was game. She shuffled her way over and was now on her back on the massage table. Now he could properly eat her. Oh

VANILLA EXTRACT

my! Lou couldn't help but moan; it was so good. Mr Fit stopped momentarily to turn up the music. Perhaps she was louder than she realised and this made her laugh inside. She couldn't help but wonder what would the other gym-goers think?

Mr Fit continued to devour her, and she was trying desperately to hold back. Lou didn't want to cum just yet. Usually it took her ages, but this experience was proving far too much fun. Normally she would have to concentrate, focusing all her thoughts on achieving the imminent explosion. This time around, however, she was fighting against it appearing too soon. Man, this was too difficult! Now she understood what men must go through when they can't help but cum too soon.

Her body was bursting at the edge of orgasm. Was it the sensual massage before? Was it because of the exciting day she'd had at the beach? It may have been because of this total surprise situation with Mr Fit? Whatever it was, she was trying to battle it, but she knew she was losing.

And there it was! EXPLOSION! She came hard. What had he done to her? Lou laid there in shock. Mr Fit was smiling above her. He could see how much Lou had relished him, but he wanted more now. "I want to fuck you," he told her. It was bold. It was simple. "Sure," she responded, still a bit flummoxed. "You have a condom?" Of course he did. He went over to a drawer and miraculously (or not) took one out. He put it on and was soon inside

VANILLA EXTRACT

her as she lay back on the massage table. God, he felt fantastic. She needed a good hard fucking now after all that build up, and he didn't disappoint her. He pounded her until he said, "Now I cum." And there it was! She held him as he unloaded inside her.

For a brief moment, they held each other. There was no real emotion or connection other than the physical interlocking. It had been a very horny encounter, but now practicalities led the way. Mr Fit withdrew and cleaned himself up. By this point, Lou was starting to come to grips with what had just transpired. This led to Lou laughing out loud and telling him how she had not expected that what so ever, and how she had thought he must be gay. "No, no. I just work here. I am not gay. I like women." He smiled as he asked her to turn over so that he could continue the massage. Lou wondered how many other women he had fooled into thinking the same as she had. 'What a player! Kudos to his tactics,' she thought.

Lou moved back onto her stomach, and Mr Fit continued to knead her muscles. It felt amazing, and she was even more relaxed now. He started on her other leg and was soon caressing her intimate areas once more. 'Could this really be happening again?' It appeared it was! Too funny! "We fuck again?" he asked. Hell yes, why not? She was impressed he was hard again so soon. Another visit to the drawer and Mr Fit was ready to take her from behind. Lou got up on her hands and knees and

VANILLA EXTRACT

arched her back as he slid inside. It felt as good as before, maybe better, because she was so sensitive inside. This time he came quicker, but she didn't mind. It was a certainly a day full of surprises.

"I *will* finish your massage," Mr Fit reassured her. Lou was as chilled out as she could ever possibly be. "You take as much time as you like," she laughed as she instructed him. He continued the massage but now focused on getting all those knots out of her back using his hands and elbows. It was a brilliant massage. Her back felt like it had really been worked and the tension was definitely gone. He'd worked miracles on her, and it was an experience she would never forget.

An hour was up, and during that time Lou felt that Mr Fit had tended to every muscle in her body, including, unexpectedly, a number of her inner ones too. Lou put on her minimal clothing and came to payment. "Surely I get a discount after that?" She joked, "In fact, you should be paying me!" Mr Fit also saw the funny side. "I will give you €10 off." Lou was happy with that. It had been a brilliant massage and a happy ending too - a delightful experience for them both.

When Lou originally thought about a massage tonight, she never quite saw it going that way. She thought she may have to have a snooze before going out in the evening, but instead Lou was buzzing to the max. Lou skipped up to her room and got ready for the final episode of her adventure before flying home the next morning. This solo travelling was proving far more fun than she ever anticipated and she would definitely do it again!

VANILLA EXTRACT

Chapter 15 – Underground Encounter

When Lou recalled this story to a number of people, a common response was received, which was - "That sounds like a film. Surely that doesn't happen in real life?" But Lou knew only too well that things like this did happen in her world. In fact, she'd had a number of similar experiences of late, so it must have been some sort of 'come get me' vibe she was emanating.

Lou had been out with her dear friend Rebecca for a spot of dinner and a good catch up. It had been a few months since they had last seen each other in person. They tended to converse via Whatsapp due to them both being busy in full-time work, had families and loved socialising. They spent a good couple of hours in Covent Garden filling each other in properly with the latest events in their respective lives. Two hours really wasn't enough, but Rebecca had to go to work and Lou had a mammoth journey back home afterwards.

They said their goodbyes and shared a heartfelt hug before they parted and went their separate ways. Lou was going to the underground station to take the tube to her car. Rebecca was catching the bus, which was just a short walk away.

VANILLA EXTRACT

At the station, Lou squeezed into the lift, descended a few floors and then walked to the platform. It was quite congested down there for a Wednesday night, but then again she was in the heart of London, where it was pretty much always busy, whatever day of the week.

The tube was quite packed, but Lou had been on worse. Try the Central Line at 8am! You can't get much crazier than that, especially on a hot, sweaty summer's day. Lou made her way into the carriage and stood at the end of the occupied seats. She was only on this line for three stops, so she really wasn't bothered about sitting down.

For anyone who has travelled on London's Underground network, they would know that it isn't usual to make eye contact, worse still to eat hot, smelly food or talk to anyone you don't know. These are some of the unwritten rules. You can glance around at people, but you have to be discrete. It's all very much a quick gander but divert your gaze as soon as you make eye contact.

Lou didn't fancy following the rules tonight. It was boring to conform on the tube. She was keen to review her surroundings and see who she was sharing her journey with this evening. Looking along the carriage to the next standing area after seats she saw a very cute young man, who happened to be staring back at her. Well, this was unusual (for most people, but Lou had experienced something similar a while back). He was very attractive, around

VANILLA EXTRACT

mid-thirties, jacket pulled in tight, scarf nestled snuggly around his neck, and enough facial hair to look enticing (rather than making her wonder what was living in all that undergrowth).

'Mmmm,' she thought. 'He's hot and cheeky too, for gawking straight at me so blatantly.' Lou held his stare for quite a bit longer than one would normally on the tube, and then looked away. She wondered if he would still be looking when she glanced back and, naturally, he was. They held this gaze for even longer this time before she looked away. Very hot indeed! She knew he would be looking the third time, and when their eyes met, Lou couldn't help but laugh. He did the same, and this was brilliant. It was one of those super special moments Lou savoured. She loved the randomness of this encounter.

Lou looked across now that some imaginary 'get to know you' line was crossed. Looking straight at him she mouthed the word 'hello.' He grinned and mouthed 'hello' back at her. They were both enjoying this game. Lou smiled too. This was fun.

Sadly, Lou's station was next, and she knew the doors would open on the other side of the carriage. She turned her body around to where she would be departing and positioned herself ready. Looking across, Lou saw him displaying an overly exaggerated shocked and then sad expression that said, 'No, don't get off.' Lou was amused, but she had to leave. She indicated that he should get off

VANILLA EXTRACT

too, by cocking her head to the side and staring at him. As she departed the train, she then wandered along the platform to the open doors opposite where he had been standing. To her surprise, she found him descending the carriage too and now standing before her. She couldn't help but smirk to herself.

"Oh wow! I didn't think you would get off," she said to this handsome stranger. "Course I got off. Why wouldn't I? A beautiful woman smiles at me on the train. I had to get off." 'Well that was rather lovely,' she thought, and then they hugged each other, like old friends meeting for the first time in a while. This was exciting and unbelievable all at once. He reached out his hand and said "Hi. I'm Michael. How are you?" Lou laughed, shook his hand and gave her name. He described where he'd been – out with friends for a few drinks. Lou did the same. "You will take my number won't you?" he asked. 'Why not?' she thought and was soon punching it into her phone. "I can't believe you smiled at me on the train. No one does that," Michael said. "Of course I did. You're gorgeous," Lou responded.

After a little more exchanging of information and compliments, it was time for them to part. They reached into each other for a hug and Lou planted a kiss on his cheek. He was grinning! They arranged to continue this excitement over Whatsapp once their phones had a signal above ground.

VANILLA EXTRACT

Lou left him waiting for the next train and made her way along the platform, only to discover she was going in completely the wrong direction. What a doughnut she was! She about-turned and said, "You didn't see that, did you?" Lou laughed as she walked past him again, now going the correct way to her next destination. She bounced her way through the station, knowing that they were both feeling pretty pleased with themselves and their encounter, as they continued their separate journeys home.

And that's where this really should have ended. It would have been a magical tale of intrigue and excitement. Tantalisingly unknowing and wanting more should have completed this desire-packed moment. However, instead, once the Whatsapp messages began, Lou soon discovered that this delectable young man had a partner at home, with a small child too. Lou chose to cease communications swiftly after. This exquisite encounter should have been left beneath the depths of London's busy streets before any lies and deceit could be raised above ground.

Chapter 16 - Italian Adventures

Scott was a gorgeous American Lou had worked with a couple of years ago. They'd met at a conference and found that they had way more in common than just their work. They had flirted subtly in front of colleagues and after a few whiskies one evening had decided to get to know each other intimately in the confines of his hotel suite. It was a naughty adventure that neither of them had expected, which made it all the more thrilling and exciting. Scott headed up a major part of the Risk division, and Lou loved his dominance and complete confidence (as a leader and in the bedroom). They spent every spare moment of that business trip together, whether at dinner, breaks and most definitely overnight. It had been a shame the conference was so short, they both agreed, but this was just the start.

Scott flew back to Sydney and Lou back to London, and it was with a tinge of sadness that they departed. There was a definite connection between them and the fuse had been lit. If their circumstances had been different, they could actually imagine making something of this newly found bond. But the reality was way different. For a start, Scott was 'happily married' and had no intention of changing that, not that Lou wanted him to. Their jobs were half a world away, and surely there would be a conflict of

VANILLA EXTRACT

interests in work terms. They decided to leave it as an exciting encounter, with brilliant memories for their respective 'wank banks'.

What this did mean though, was that any time their paths crossed again for work reasons, should he be visiting the UK, or when she was asked to go to Sydney, that they would naturally pick up where they left off and have a crazy few days, nights or even stolen hours together, which inevitably meant getting naked and ravenously taking their fill.

Over a period of four years, before he left the company, they stayed in touch periodically and tended to make contact as and when business trips were being confirmed. On this basis, they coordinated their whereabouts and just so happened to be in the same place at the same time in London on a few occasions, once in Dubai and another time in New York. Lou loved the associated build-up and adrenalin buzz as the planning came to fruition for each of those out of the ordinary adventures. Meeting him in a foreign land fuelled the excitement, although even on her home ground, she would be chomping at the bit to see him!

Lou felt it was a shame when his career led him off to 'pursue other opportunities' and she was hesitant to contact him outside of work's internal systems in case it caused any issues at home. They had become friends on Facebook, but kept it very low key. The odd like of a photo or quote was about as far as the interaction went. She was pleased then when she

VANILLA EXTRACT

saw a picture posted of him eating pasta and drinking wine near the Leaning Tower of Pisa in Italy. She immediately liked the Facebook entry and added, "Looks like you're having fun!" Lou was surprised then to see her phone ringing almost instantly via Facebook and there he was, talking to her for the first time in a few months.

"There she is," he began. Lou was thrilled. She always maintained a soft spot where Scott was concerned. Whether that was because she couldn't have him, she wasn't sure, but he just had a way of making her feel special, and she soaked it up. He stimulated her mentally as well as physically, and this was all-important. Sex was great, as it could be with many different people, but if you don't have that intellect and humour, then it can be very mechanical, Lou had discovered, so Scott ticked many boxes for her.

They were on the phone for over an hour that Sunday evening. He told her how his new job had taken him to Italy and he would be based there for the next three weeks. This sparked her imagination. Italy was way closer than Australia and many other places he had worked. It was also a short flight away from where she lived (which also happened to be very close to where a number of budget airlines operated out of). "What are you doing at the weekend then?" Lou enquired, hoping he would say that his new employer had nothing scheduled for him. "I have no plans whatsoever. Why? What are you plotting?" Scott asked, now wondering what

VANILLA EXTRACT

she had in mind. "Well if you would like some company, I could easily jump on a plane for the weekend and come join you." It took no time whatsoever for Scott to respond, "I would absolutely love that." And so the plan was hatched.

Come Friday afternoon, Lou found herself checked in on the 17:50 to Pisa. It was a bargain flight, returning at 22:30 on the Sunday. This gave them two full days and nights together in a land they had not shared before. The plan was for Scott to meet her at the Italian airport and whisk her away to his hotel.

The flight really couldn't go quickly enough. It seemed to drag so very slowly as Lou imagined what their meeting would be like. Would it be like in the movies, where she would run to greet him and be lifted in the air and spun around? More likely he'd be stuck in traffic, and she'd be sat on a bench for ages waiting for him to show! How reality had a way of bringing you down to earth!

With just a small trolley dolly and no luggage checked in, Lou was able to go straight through passport control and into arrivals, and there he was, standing tall and magnificent, waiting for her. Just as she remembered, he was looking gorgeous as ever. Sporting very casual attire, his denim jeans and open shirt made her want to go and lick him all over, but that probably wasn't appropriate, not even here, where signs of affection were more welcomed than other European cities.

VANILLA EXTRACT

"There you are Lou Lou." They both rushed in and lips were on each other's before they could say anymore. The embrace that followed was heartfelt and meaningful. Despite the miles and the months, this always felt right. "Hello you," she said when they released their hold. "Hello to you too," he tried in his most posh English accent, that sounded more like Dick van Dyke than she cared to let on. It just reminded her that despite his 6' 4", he was still a little cutie at times.

Scott took Lou's bag and escorted her, arm in arm, to his hire car. Before they knew it, they were parked up at the hotel and making their way to his room. Once inside, Scott asked her what she'd like to drink. Given the late hour of her arrival, Scott had prepared a bedroom picnic. There were crisps, nuts, cheeses, chocolate and cakes, as well as her favourite tipple of gin and tonic. He'd thought of everything!

Instead of jumping each other's bones there and then, they spent the next four hours getting reacquainted. It had been over a year since they had seen one another, so they took their time eating and drinking and chatting about their lives, including jobs, children, relationships, work and a whole plethora of other subjects. They were shocked to find out the time when they drew breath to have a look.

While his room was a twin, Scott had left the table and lamp in between both beds as they had been happily talking on the sofas. Lou had spotted this

VANILLA EXTRACT

set up as soon as she'd entered his room but didn't say anything. She initially wondered if this trip would see them sleeping separately for the first time, but perhaps just enjoying the company instead. They did make each other laugh and found each other fascinating, so it could be that this time would be non-physical. In fact, they didn't approach the subject until it was time to turn in.

"So what's the set up here exactly?" Lou asked him directly. "Are we gonna move that table out of the way then?" In Lou's mind, she hadn't flown all this way not to have him naked in bed. Scott was ever polite and a gentleman. "Well, I didn't want to presume that was what you had in mind, but I'm glad you did." He eagerly moved the lamp and then table across and slid both beds together. "That's better!"

It was quite extraordinary to have spent all that time getting to know someone again, reconnecting and catching up on respective lives and being completely honourable, to then be slipping out of your clothes and passionately kissing that very same person with an uncontrollable and insatiable lust! Having gone from being a little tipsy and tired to now wide awake and wanting! How quickly your body can change so dramatically from one extreme to the other.

Standing on tiptoe, Lou was being kissed deeply. She loved this. How he held her close as his tongue plunged inside. His right arm was around her back pulling her in, as his left hand held the back of her

VANILLA EXTRACT

head. She felt ripples run through her entire being. She was so turned on. He led her to the bed and continuing to kiss her, pushed her gently back. As she lay down, he was on her. He was ripe and ready. His desire was strong, and she was going to get it. His hands were on her jeans' zip, and they were coming down rapidly. Slipping them towards the floor, where she was kicking her boots off, he left the trousers around her ankles with her knickers. Scott firmly placed his head between her legs and began his feast. His need was strong, and Lou was happy to oblige. She adored his passion.

Despite the long day, travel, alcohol and talking, Lou surprised herself and let go quite quickly of the built-up tensions within her body. His excitement and superb tongue skills had her exploding all over the place before she had even really thought about it. God, he felt good. Just like he always did. It was time for him to get inside her. Unlike times gone by, both were now a little more responsible than they had been in their earlier encounters, and they each had condoms at the ready. So much for them not expecting any action, eh?

When Scott was deep inside her, she felt instantly complete once more. He had a habit of making her feel this way, despite their time apart. It was magical. They picked up exactly where they left off each time and it amazed them both that it could be this way - brilliant in fact. (Not that this was the only person who Lou felt this connection with, but she enjoyed it all the same). Maybe keeping it to

VANILLA EXTRACT

this level of regularity meant the light would never dim on this arrangement and perhaps it could outlive many others as it was kept at a slow burning low ebb, with the occasional roaring fire from time to time?

After an hour of love-making, they fell asleep in each other's arms, again unusual for Lou but for some reason, this felt right. Normally she would want her own space to sleep and make her way away from a lover.

After probably not long enough, given her previous day and the even longer night, they woke pretty much in the same position and started up again from where they left off. It was just as wild as the night before and even more messy, as they let themselves relax more. With a whole weekend together 24/7, she had a feeling they'd be spending most of it nakedly entwined, and that was just fine by them both!

They were too late for breakfast, so showered and made their way into Pisa. They should at least take in some scenery while she was there. The tower was beautiful, and they took the obligatory tourist shots of holding it up as it leaned into them. Tacky as it was, it gave them both a laugh, particularly when other visitors were taking it all so seriously.

With little else to see there, Scott suggested taking a train to Florence, and within two hours they found themselves exploring another city, which was far

VANILLA EXTRACT

more picturesque. Lou took a number of photographs as she was so taken aback with the architecture and stunning art. She found the place so captivating that it didn't look real. This weekend certainly was becoming an adventure for Lou, and that was before she accompanied Scott to his first ever swingers club that evening.

Lou spoke with the Italian couple she met in Gran Canaria earlier in the year. They recommended a club just outside of the city where they often went for fun, with friends and tourists alike. Luca arranged for their names to be on the guest list and asked the owner to give them a tour when they arrived and to generally look after them. Unfortunately, they would not be able to join them that evening as Maria had recently had knee surgery and was out of action for a while.

During lunch in the most beautiful Piazza Della Signoria, they discussed their evening's plans. Scott was keen to have a cover story for anyone they spoke with at the club. Over pasta, they came up with their elaborate fabrication. Lou allegedly had a very rich father, potentially famous but undecided at this stage, who was in need of security protection. Being his daughter, Lou had to be accompanied at all times to avoid the threat of kidnap and ransom being demanded. Their scheming developed as they thought more about this scenario, while trying to keep it believable.

Scott had been with the family for seven years and

VANILLA EXTRACT

more closely with Lou for the past two. In protecting her, he had to travel wherever she went, and on this occasion, Florence was where Lou decided she wanted to visit. His hotel room was next door to hers, and there was an adjoining door to allow swift access if she had an intruder that needed to be 'sorted'.

Scott was ex-military and used to dressing pristinely so he decided he would be staying in his suit at the club. Given he looked super hot in a smart suit, Lou was very happy that he would be adorning this attire. (Secretly, he was a little uneasy baring all and was shy about his body, and therefore this excuse worked perfectly. Lou couldn't quite understand why. He had a lovely body.)

The taxi picked them up at 8pm and Lou sat behind the driver, as advised by her security attachment. Scott told her this was the safest place for her to be in the car. The role-play had already commenced and who was she to question his expertise? Their journey took around 40 minutes, and across parts of the city and outskirts, she wasn't sure she'd like to travel around alone.

Lou was surprised at the location when they finally pulled up. It was an industrial park and the club appeared to be next to a car repair centre. The only evidence that gave away its presence was a small sign next to a doorbell that said *Eroticas* in bright red capital letters. A camera was already watching them as they rang it. A few seconds later the door

VANILLA EXTRACT

automatically opened and they walked inside.

Immediately ahead of them was the reception area where Lola greeted them. She gave them a huge pink glossy smile as she welcomed them. Dressed in a tight cerise sequinned frock and even brighter long ponytailed wig, she said, "Ciao, ciao," and then continued on very quickly in Italian. Scott, fortunately, knew some Italian, but Lou didn't, and she stared blankly for a moment. Scott explained that they spoke little Italian and Lola switched straight to English to carry on. When she ticked their names off the list, she realised who they were. "Ok, you are friends of Luca and Maria. Welcome. I will show you my club. I hope that you love it as much as they do."

Lou had already spotted that Lola's Adam's Apple was rather large for a female and guessed that Lola hadn't started life wearing dresses. She also noticed her amazing shoes and felt instant footwear envy. They were gloriously high and made Lola's legs look fantastic. Lola tottered around, overly flamboyant and so much mischief too. Her humour was very funny as she explained the different rooms and contents for club-goers' enjoyment and thrills.

There were some rooms where you could close the doors, which Lou thought Scott might favour more, given his shyness around other people. The open play area was sectioned off with prison-like bars, so you could watch all the action (or be watched, as Lou preferred). There were also cushions dotted

VANILLA EXTRACT

around the padded floor for comfort. Another room had restraints in the walls, a love swing and a chair with inbuilt stirrups. The suede vault looked like it had seen plenty of action, though not of the traditional gymnastic variety.

On the ground floor, the wet area was enormous. A large jacuzzi was bubbling away empty at this point, inviting swingers to enter and take pleasure in the water. Next to this was a huge sauna room with clear glass and three levels of seating. There were toilets and open showers here too.

Along from here was another area with a pole and surrounding leather seating for viewing any demonstration and playing. Upstairs from this was a padded mezzanine area looking out to the action below, but equally becoming an additional stage, if desired.

Walking back to the U-shaped bar area now, Lola showed them where they could get any drink they wished and also showed them where the dance floor and DJ could be found. Nobody was dancing yet, but there were plenty of people already soaking up the atmosphere. Another pole was in the middle of the dance area and Lou thought she'd be bound to have a go on that after a few drinks. Lola was also a pole lover, she laughed as she told them and then gave them a one-handed spin as she walked past it. She certainly had good upper body strength!

Moving then to the locker area Lola said, "You can

put your clothes in here." She smiled at Scott and gave him a wink. "No need to carry anything about with you. Your drinks and food are included in the price. There is no photography, so leave your phones here, please. I will leave you now. Get naked, have fun and find me if you need anything. I mean anything!" Again she smiled directly at Scott and minced off back to reception. She was playful. Lou liked it, but she thought Scott felt a little uncomfortable with her.

Lou placed her bag in the locker, along with her jacket. She wouldn't change yet into the sexy red lace dress Scott had chosen but would have a drink first. Scott didn't want to disrobe at all and was happy to keep his full suit on for now. They made their way to the bar and ordered a gin and tonic for her and a Jack Daniels and Coke for him. Both drinks went down very smoothly as they perused the club's attendees already there and new joiners as they came in. Scott was like a sponge, absorbing every detail. This was a scenario completely alien to him, and it was taking a while to process. Fortunately, Lou had been to similar places and could answer his questions with experienced answers. This (and the Jack Daniels) helped to settle any concerns, and he became a little more relaxed.

There were a few couples at the bar, and Lou was pleased that the quality of appearances was of a high standard. There were some very good-looking people there including some single men. It didn't take long for one of them to strike up a conversation, firstly

VANILLA EXTRACT

with Scott, which was the respectful thing to do. His name was Tom, and he was asking if it was their first time to *Eroticas.* He had obviously heard their accents, albeit one English and one American. And so the small talk began. Tom was actually from Stuttgart in Germany and was here on business. It was now time for Scott and Lou to test out their imaginary relationship and find out if it was believable. It flowed very effortlessly. A few captured smiles and affectionate caresses added to the impression, even though they came very naturally and didn't need to be put on.

Lou wasn't sure whether Tom bought any of their story or if he was just humouring this crazy couple before him, with the intention of having hot sex with her. As the conversation continued, Lou was finding it fascinating that Scott was equally comfortable recalling apparent events they had both shared over the past few years together. This was amusing, and Lou wondered how thick this web of harmless deceit would grow before it became ridiculous.

When Tom took himself off to the toilet, Scott asked Lou if she wanted to find somewhere for the three of them to play? Was she comfortable with Tom joining them? He seemed like a nice guy from the interaction they'd had so far and Lou agreed. They would have another drink together first before he approached Tom with this proposition.

Lou decided it was time to lose some clothing as the

VANILLA EXTRACT

thought of pleasure was making her hot. She went off to the locker room and changed into the full-length dress. It had a halter neck and split from the right side of the waist right down to the floor. The side was then loosely tied together with a red silk thin ribbon, exposing everything underneath it. The stretchy lace gave a similar effect. You could see through it, but it had elegance as well as naughtiness. It hugged her slim figure beautifully, and she felt confident in this sophisticated, yet cheeky attire.

When she returned to the room, a few heads turned as she walked in. Perfect: just the reaction she was looking for. Scott saw all of this, soaking in the atmosphere as his woman engulfed herself in the limelight. He had been engrossed in conversation with Tom until this point, but Lou earned his attention immediately. His gorgeous eyes were sparkling even more than usual. "You look stunning," Tom leaned in to tell her. "Thank you," Lou graciously replied. "Wow, babe. You're beautiful. That dress was definitely the right choice. It fits in all the right places. I can't wait to fuck you in it!" Lou felt an instant twinge. Damn, she was horny. "Go put your clothes away. I'll be waiting here for you." Scott didn't even respond. He grabbed the locker key from her and was gone in a shot!

Lou and Tom continued their conversation. It was now more focused on sex clubs and what each other enjoyed. Tom often went to clubs in Germany,

VANILLA EXTRACT

where the atmosphere was very relaxed. It was very acceptable in and around Stuttgart and people would happily travel there for the club he mentioned. Lou said the same that she had found clubs outside of London could be as much fun, and sometimes more than those in the city centre.

Scott returned. Now down to his pants, he said, "Tom, we're going to go find somewhere to relax. Would you like to join us?" Tom looked genuinely surprised. "Of course I would. I would love to join you." He looked at Lou, almost reassuring himself that she was comfortable with this arrangement and it was not being forced upon her. Lou was smiling back at him. Oh, she was more than happy.

Scott led the way to a room where the door could be closed. As his first time, he wanted to ease himself in and not be too worried about other people joining them. Lou wanted him to feel comfortable and savour every moment of his initiation. They went into a room that had a small purpose-built leather bed. It allowed the person lying horizontally to have access all round. One end accommodated legs being splayed, while the other end had a dipped head area. It looked awkward to get into, but once Lou was in position, it all made sense!

Tom was first to go down on Lou and he was very keen to make her cum. At the other end, Scott stood facing the bed. The head position Lou found herself in was perfect for sucking his cock and balls. The groaning began, but it wasn't from Lou. It was from

VANILLA EXTRACT

Scott. He loved the sensation of her oral skills, but watching Lou being licked out was turning him on at the same time. It was a double sensation that was exciting him more than he'd ever expected. "Oh baby, that's so good!" Lou felt the same. Giving and receiving in unison was super tingly, and she knew she was already starting to cum, albeit the slow continued stream type, rather than the mind-blowing crescendo variety.

Tom was lapping furiously and Lou had to tell him to slow it down. He apologised. "I am so very excited. You taste so good. I want to please you." He was also sweating profusely. "Let me go take a quick shower." He withdrew and headed out to the shower room next door. Scott decided to take up the now vacant position and began to stroke her slowly with his tongue. Having this different technique so soon was sending her to higher levels and her sighs began rhythmically. Lou had to grab onto the sides to steady herself, as she let out a more explosive orgasm. "That's right baby. Let me have it." She did. It was supercharged and she unloaded instantly over his face. After the initial scream of euphoria, Lou said, "Mmmm, so good. Thank you!" It was more of a pant or whisper than a full voice. It was all that would come out of her mouth at the time.

Lou hadn't noticed Tom return. He had watched her cum and was now massaging his very excited penis. He kneeled next to Scott, and the tongues swapped again. This prolonged her cumming and despite the intense currents running through her body, she could feel herself building up again. Oh boy. This was unreal. Lou always came quicker the second time (and third, and fourth, and more). It was Tom's turn now. His fingers were inside her and he was digging deep. Lou was gasping louder, and there it was. Only this time it was gush and Tom was covered! Splashing ensued as he continued rigorously and he was saturated! Oh wow. Everyone now was a little shocked! They hadn't foreseen it going quite this way, but they were all happy it had! Ever resourceful, Tom gave Lou the towel he had returned from the shower in.

Scott had been watching this with intent. "Baby, I really need to be inside you." Lou immediately changed positions and was now in doggy style, waiting for him to take her. Tom headed to the other end, and Lou took him in her mouth. His cock wasn't as long as Scott's, but it had girth. She had to be careful not to injure him as Scott put a condom on and slid inside her slowly. With her recovering vagina still convulsing, the sensation was even more heightened. This was absolutely amazing.

Scott began to pump her hard. It was what they both needed at this point. Lou backed into him equally as ferociously and grabbed his arse with her right hand. She felt her nails dig in and it made Scott let out an animalistic growl. She knew he could cum at any moment. At the same time, Tom was moaning with pleasure and congratulated her

VANILLA EXTRACT

on her technique.

To stop himself from orgasm, Scott withdrew from her. "I don't want to cum yet. I want to watch Tom fuck you." "Sure. Why not?" Lou waited for the guys to swap positions and soon found Scott in her mouth now instead, having whipped off the condom in the transition. Tom had put some protection on and was fucking her slowly to start. It was very soon that he had sped up and was slamming her harder. Scott was looking closely. While enjoying Lou's tongue, he was fascinated to watch her being fucked. There were all sorts of angles he saw that he could never experience as the person usually doing the penetrating (he would later tell her). It was turning him on as much to watch as to fuck Lou.

This arrangement seemed to be working for both men. Tom was now groaning loudly and said he would soon have to cum. This seemed to give Scott extra inspiration to do the same. It would have been such a porn film moment if they had both cum together, but that wasn't the case, although close. Tom was first, giving a massive yell, "Oh Mein Gott. Ich komme!" 'Well, that was easy enough to understand!' Lou thought given she spoke no German herself. It was the trigger Scott needed. "Oh baby, baby it's coming. I'm so close. Oh yeah, yeah, YEAH!" That was it. Scott had shot his load all over her breasts and was standing holding his emptied cock. It was a double whammy with the cumming, with grunts at both ends, soon to be

VANILLA EXTRACT

replaced with calm. Lou was thrilled to be at the centre of this exciting entanglement.

As usual, her laughter began, which then led to both men chuckling too. It was Scott who congratulated Tom on his performance. "Good effort Tom. You were awesome!" Tom, now covered in sweat once more and very much out of breath, thanked Scott. "I need another shower!" Tom kissed Lou and told her she had been wonderful too. He would meet them back at the bar once he'd freshened up. That worked for them all. Scott rubbed the hot spunk all over Lou's tits as she instructed him too, massaging it in as he caressed her. Lou let out a "Phew," of her own, and they made their way to the showers.

Scott wondered if they should get dressed once they had refreshed themselves, but Lou advised they could drink in the bar area with their towels on. He seemed surprised but then quite comfortable as he saw most other guests were down to towels now throughout the club. Just how much time had passed since they had been playing with Tom? It had only felt like a short time but well over an hour and a half had disappeared before them.

At the bar, they had more drinks. They had earned them. Both feeling a bit peckish, they decided to go for some food. However, neither of them particularly fancied eating a full meal from the buffet being offered. Instead, Tom advised there were crepes being made in the outdoor section, so that's where they headed. It seemed a little surreal, being post-coital with the two men she had just fucked, to now be eating a Nutella and banana crepe and chatting about life in general. How funny, yet so natural!

The snack went down a treat, and they moved back to the bar area. Tom had to leave as he had an early start the next day. They bid farewell, thanked each other for the good time and Tom and Scott exchanged numbers. Whether they would remain in contact was unknown. This just seemed to be the polite thing to do.

After Tom departed, it wasn't long before a couple approached them, asking if they wanted to play. Lou was very conscious that, being Scott's first time in a club, the decision would really be with him. They were both lovely looking, which wasn't always the case with couples. Normally one of the two would be gorgeous, while the other not quite so blessed. It could mean one of your party would 'take one for the team' if that was your agreement, but Lou wasn't into that, and she wouldn't expect Scott (or any of her partners) to be so either. She was also aware that he would have to consider recovery time, and if he'd even be up for another round. Was his body ready or fit enough to go again? Fortunately, he was, so game on!

Chiara was 32 and her partner Giulio was 34. She had bleached, long blonde hair and enormous breasts; at least an H cup implant. Her frame was petite otherwise, and her towel could have wrapped

VANILLA EXTRACT

around her twice if it hadn't been for those huge puppies. Giulio was around 5' 11", slim and toned rather than bulky and muscly. They were regulars at the club and only lived 20 minutes away.

Chiara, despite her size, was very forthright. She asked if Lou was into girls, to which she responded positively. Chiara went on to say that she had only recently discovered her bisexual side and would like to taste Lou if Lou was willing. This sent shivers down Lou's spine. An offer she would rarely turn down! With this and a nod from Lou, Chiara took her hand and led her away from the bar to play. The gents followed eagerly.

The ladies made their way to a room with one-way glass. This meant that people could stand outside the room and watch, with those in the room not feeling that they were being spied upon. This was a little disappointing for Lou, as she liked to know she had an audience and to gauge their reactions to her performance. Equally though, she knew Scott would find this arrangement better suiting, so she happily went with the flow.

The towels were soon discarded as Chiara and Lou lay on the bed. Lou was asked to go onto her back so she could be tasted. Both men stood at the edge of the bed to view this and were fascinated with what they saw. Lou had found that men enjoy watching women very much, especially when pussies were being licked and that's what was beginning here. First, the ladies kissed softly, caressing each

VANILLA EXTRACT

other's breasts and holding their heads together, their hands running through the hair as they gently slid tongues inside mouths. Both were smiling intently and enjoying every tingly moment. Chiara was squeezing Lou's breast as she made her way to her groin area. It was very sensual, and Lou's back was already arching in delight as she emitted her first sighs of this encounter.

For an alleged novice, Chiara knew exactly what she was doing. Her tongue was gentle to start as it explored her magical area. She began to build up a rhythm around her clit, and Lou soon began to grind against her face. At the same time, she caught a glimpse of Scott. She had almost forgotten the men were even in the room, as she lost herself in the moment. They too were naked and were separately massaging their own cocks as they watched the girl on girl show evolving before them.

Lou indicated for them to join in. Giulio stood before the bed so that Lou could take his manhood in her mouth, which she was only too pleased to do. Scott headed towards Chiara and slipped a finger inside her as she continued to devour Lou. They were all now moving together in this delicious connection.

Lou was over the moon with her lot. Giulio was even bigger than Scott, and she couldn't wait to get him inside her. She wondered how he would compare with Scott, who was already a fantastic ride. Chiara would certainly not be disappointed.

VANILLA EXTRACT

Lou pulled Chiara to her face so that she could kiss her deeply and taste herself on her lips. "I hope I was sweet enough for you," she enquired. "Absolutely delightful," Chiara responded and licked her lips purposefully. It was time to swap around. The girls, now split apart, were focusing on the new partners they were about to experience fully. Giulio continued to have his cock sucked by Lou and Chiara spun onto her back, so she could watch Scott playing with her. Lou made eye contact with Scott and read that he was full of desire. He was certainly very happy to continue. 'Good,' she thought. Let the games begin!

Lou stepped up the pace on the member she was bringing oral delight to. Back and forth, like a wave, she built the rhythm, but what she really wanted was to feel Giulio inside her. His cock had a slight kink in it, and she was curious to how different it would be compared to Scott's. Giulio on the other hand was happily moaning with her mouth wrapped around him. Lou withdrew and motioned for him to join her on the bed. She slithered back up the bed, so he could see what she wanted. However, Giulio thought that meant to return the tongue skills and immediately buried his head between her thighs. "Oh go on then," she said out loud and laughed.

At this point, she saw Scott put a condom on and enter Chiara. There were gasps of pleasure to Lou's left as they were locked together and the pounding began. Lou reached over and grabbed Chiara's

VANILLA EXTRACT

nearest breast and gave the nipple a gentle tweak. It was like nothing Lou had ever experienced – the noise that is! It sounded like Chiara was being murdered! The volume was through the roof, and it wasn't relenting. "OOOOOHHH, AAAAHHHH, YESSSSSS!" Scott looked down at Lou for assistance, but there was nothing she could do. She retracted her hand from boob caressing, but this did nothing to stop the screeching. Lou shrugged her shoulders and smiled, "When in Rome and all that!" Technically, there weren't in Rome, but close enough!

Trying to put the banshee noises out of her mind, Lou focused on the tongue she was receiving. It was quite difficult to concentrate with all of this racket going on, so Lou made her mind up that she wasn't likely to come. Instead, she would go for the same option as Scott. A jolly good pounding was in order, and Giulio was just the man to give it to her.

At the same time, Lou decided she wanted the door opened. It was getting very hot inside, plus she was sure people would have been watching. She did love the attention, and now Lou wanted to see if their steamy ensemble had drawn a crowd.

Reaching across to the side shelf, Lou took a condom and handed it to him. "Giulio, please get inside me!' He did as he was asked and then slowly slid his huge penis inside her. "Mmmm," she sighed, quietly by comparison, as he did and continued, "Ooh, that does feel good!"

VANILLA EXTRACT

The mixed-up couples were now next to each other on the bed, going at it separately, which oddly became in time, as the fucking continued. As well as watching the show, it was probably Chiara's noises that brought other voyeurs to the room. Some were probably there to make sure she was ok and others because her screams had turned them on. She was like an alarm going off!

Around the edge of the bed, couples were standing and watching as they played with each other. Lou spotted others' hands touching and fingering partners and general acknowledgement of the horny scene in front of them. Another couple ventured onto the bed and began to join in. Both gorgeous with fit bodies, they were well suited to those already entwined. It was time again for a swap around, or so they had hoped.

Just as they were working out who was going where there was a call from outside the room. Lola was strutting around in those same glorious shoes and sequined ensemble. The club would be closing in 15 minutes. Damn! Where had this evening gone? Had time sped up? Did this always happen in clubs? Lou was convinced it must do.

Inside the room, it meant they would have to decide if they would be able to fully enjoy this now orgy-like atmosphere. Scott looked like his mind was set on pounding Chiara to the point of cumming. This could be for his self-gratification or to shut her up! Either way, he was on a mission and getting faster and faster. Only when he came did her squawks subside and were replaced by equally loud whimpers. It was an improvement Lou thought.

Giulio was smiling at Lou. "My wife is very loud, no?" 'Bloody right,' Lou thought. She was beyond loud! Lou sank her tongue deep into Giulio's mouth and then pulled away. Time was not on their side, so she asked him if he was likely to come. He looked perplexed initially until Lou said, "If you are going to come, then you need to do it now. Are you going to come now for me Giulio?" He nodded sheepishly. "Then do it!" This masterful instruction was enough to send him to the point of no return. He was excited by her moment of dominance and almost instantly came on the spot. The truth was that Lou was not too fussed about rushing a further orgasm for herself. If she wanted that, then she'd jump on Scott again when they returned to their hotel. At this point, she just wanted to get dressed so they could head off!

As the club closed, Giulio and Scott exchanged numbers and pleasantries, as did Lou and Chiara. Similar to Tom, Lou wondered if they would ever stay in touch. It really didn't matter. She doubted she would ever see any of them again.

As the club closed, they made their way back to the hotel; reminiscing about the adventures they had experienced this evening. Tonight was more about making lifelong memories than friends, and they had definitely achieved this objective.

VANILLA EXTRACT

The next day was a lazy day, and they did not rise until lunchtime. Lou was ravenous, for food as well as sex. She couldn't get her head around the fact that however much sex she had, she always wanted more. It was like a drug: the more you had, the more you wanted. Either that or she was just a greedy cow! Although men had told her they were wired the same way. Who says you can't have too much of a good thing? It seems you can, until you want more, of course!

Despite her hunger, Lou found herself enjoying a rather prolonged sensual experience as she woke. Scott's dampened finger was ever so slightly caressing her clitoris. It was delicate, and it was slow as it moved across the tip. There was no pressure and none was needed. Damn this guy knows his stuff! So many men think that you have to go hard and vigorous to arouse this delightful bean. Instead, Scott had activated her 'tap', or rather this was how she chose to describe it. Lou was able to come from this stimulation, but a different form of orgasm to the fanfare type. She thought it was like a tap dripping ever so slightly as the cumming continued. It could go on and on, and the tingling sensation would grow and grow. She loved it. Why oh why did so few men know how to do this? End that with a little force and the full-on exploding type would follow. Divine, if you asked Lou!

Lou's moans, crescendo and mess had turned him on, and he had been ready for ages before she climbed on board his erection. She rode him deep, and her pulsating vagina was like a tingling web of electrodes surrounding him as he came inside her. Wow!

What a shame she only had two days with him. Any more and they would have to hibernate, call room service and probably need some form of resuscitation!

He later dropped her back at the airport, where there were fond farewells, hugs and kisses. They had no idea when their paths would cross again, or where for that matter. It had been a magical weekend, one that neither of them would forget.

VANILLA EXTRACT

Chapter 17 – Rules of Disengagement

Another swinging house party this time, and Lou was going to be accompanied by 'Pants' as her partner. She was excited when he picked her up from her house. They had met a few times socially since their first encounter, for lunch and for drinks but still, they had not had sex. Tonight was going to be the night, at the same location their paths originally crossed a few months before.

The theme for tonight's gathering was 'leather and lace' and Lou had the perfect outfit sorted, which was neither of those fabrics, but sexy all the same. It was a leatherette mini dress, and we are talking barely covering her peachy bottom. The front was complimented with zigzag zips woven through it. The thin spaghetti straps on any other dress would either sit on top of bra straps, or Lou would wear a strapless one underneath. But at this sort of party, one didn't really worry if your nipples were erect and showed through! Lou had it packed to change into at the hotel.

They arranged to meet at 7.30pm. Lou was convinced he would try it on with her before the party, which wasn't kicking off till 9pm, albeit an hours drive away, via The Red Lion pub and guest house. As it transpired, Pants was late. She later found this was the norm with him, but this was the first time she'd experienced his tardiness. He messaged her at 7.30pm to say he was a bit behind but on route. He finally showed up some 40 minutes later. (Lou didn't know him well enough at this point to have a moan about his lateness, so he had no idea how she loathed it.)

All was forgiven when he arrived looking rather dapper and smelling divine. As his E Class Mercedes pulled up on her drive, Lou made her way downstairs. He was at the front door waiting. Lou had tight jeans on, a baggy top and Converse. Her hair was neatly straightened, and her make-up done. (She'd had plenty of time to check and double check.) She had even gone with a smoky eye effect, just because she had some extra time to experiment, and was pleased with the result. "I'll change when we get there. Don't worry; this isn't my outfit!" Pants was aware of that but made a joke, rounded off with, "You'd look beautiful in anything." What a charmer!

Pants drove them to the hotel. It was surprisingly better than Lou had anticipated. He had booked a suite, with a queen size bed and en-suite with a high backed free-standing bath. 'All very posh,' Lou thought. It was a shame they didn't have time to use the facilities now. She changed into the dress, put on some glossy black hold-ups with lace tops and then her Mary Jane heels. (They were a pair of her work shoes, but no one was likely to know.) Pants changed into his leather kilt, tight black t-shirt, and

VANILLA EXTRACT

he was ready to go. It was a good look. It suited him.

"God Lou. You look amazing. Maybe we should just stay in tonight?" Pants said with a cheeky smile. If they didn't have the party to go to and her friends to meet there, then that would have been a very viable option. But Lucy, Rebecca, Sabrina and Karen were meeting her there, and she didn't like to let people down. Pants was also looking forward to seeing them and getting to know them all intimately if he could - such was his sexual appetite. What a tart!

Lou messaged the girlie group chat and informed them they were running late. They'd be at the party for 10pm and that was just fine, given Lucy was waiting for a 'cub' to arrive before they set off. (She always had a penchant for younger men.) They agreed to meet in the house, and there was no real stress about the actual time they convened. No one had dropped out, so that was good as it had been a while since the ladies were last 'on tour.'

Pants and Lou had a cheeky gin and tonic before their cab arrived. He'd picked up a few of the premixed cans before he'd collected Lou. Forward-thinking too - she was impressed! It went down a treat. She didn't realise how much she fancied a drink.

While they were waiting for the cab, they discussed their 'terms of engagement.' Considering it was their

VANILLA EXTRACT

first party as a couple, what did that actually mean? Would they just stay and play together? Would they do that but introduce other people who took their fancy? Would they just go in together and reconvene at the end of the night? This was unchartered territory for them together - different if attending separately, of course. They agreed to play as a couple and see if anyone else was fit enough to join them later. Lou was happy with that arrangement. She wanted him first, given they had unfinished business, so that was perfect - the best of both!

Arriving at the party, they were greeted by the hosts and handed a complimentary glass of champagne. They made their way into the kitchen and found Rebecca waiting with her guest Chris. 'He's a real cutie,' Lou thought, 'she'd kept him quiet.' Lou thought Rebecca was coming alone but was certainly glad now that she'd turned up with this delightful specimen. Next to them both was Sabrina, who ran up and gave Lou a cuddle. That was sweet. She introduced a fair skinned beauty called Karen, who Lou had not met before, and the circle was almost complete.

Just as they were unpacking the cans of drink and putting them in the fridge, Lucy made a grand entrance behind them. "Where's my favourite MILF then?" She was referring to Lou, and she marched over, squeezed her bum and gave Lou a massive hug. "How have you been, you old strumpet?" Lucy was always the life and soul of the party and tonight was

VANILLA EXTRACT

no exception. She'd brought with her a toned, gorgeous 30-year-old hunk called Sam, who didn't look quite sure what he'd let himself in for.

After group reconnections were made, all suitably kissed and compliments on outfits exchanged, they took a wander around the house. It was time for a tour, not to get familiar with the surroundings, but more to see if any action was taking place and what other talent was available for later possibilities.

They only got as far as upstairs in the bedroom they'd had fun in last time they were here. This time the scenario played out differently. It took on a new path as the ladies were excited and the raucous laughter increased. Initially, they were chatting and giggling, but this soon turned into a full-on show for anyone else in the room or passing through. It started with kissing and then some caressing, and before they knew it, the action began.

With the ladies almost pack-like to begin, Pants, Chris and Sam were watching and waiting in the wings. As soon as Lucy and Sabrina started kissing, they moved in. To Lou's surprise, Pants was straight there as Lucy moved over to kiss Sam deeply. He was behind her, kissing her neck as Sam immediately got his cock out and started fucking her standing there. Pants, having received the low down from Lou prior to the party, knew that Lucy was partial to anal sex, and he began to give her just that. 'Bloody hell,' Lou thought. 'He doesn't waste any time. And what exactly happened to us having each

VANILLA EXTRACT

other first?' Lou let it go, but she wasn't impressed.

Pants had effectively given her the green light to have her own fun, as the group moved around like some party game where a chair is removed on each round. Rebecca and Lou were kissing Chris, and he went down on Lou as Rebecca then sucked him off. Sam then joined them. He'd lost momentum with Pants pounding Lucy and was now stroking his penis near Lou's head. She helped him out by putting it in her mouth and he was soon rock hard again. As she looked over at Pants, she could see he and Lucy were moving to a bed for more comfort and she was now giving him oral pleasure.

Sabrina and Karen were talking on the bed before Lucy engaged them in more kissing. Karen had a master who wasn't present, and she was not allowed to play with any other male. Females, however, were acceptable, so she soon got involved with the other girls. Pants moved onto Sabrina as Lucy pulled out her bag of tricks and located her strap-on. It was time to make sure Karen enjoyed her night as much as the others, with or without her Sir.

Lou meanwhile now had Chris pounding her vagina as Sam was fucking her mouth. Ding, ding - time to swap again. Just as well there were plenty of condoms already in the rooms. They were getting through them at a rate of knots, although none of the men were ejaculating. She knew Pants was unlikely to. He enjoyed a Viagra buzz and preferred to fuck as many different women as possible on a night off from his missus. He wasn't too fussed about cumming as such, well not until the end of the night.

Chris was now with Rebecca, Pants fucking Sabrina, Lucy making Karen cum and Sam probing Lou. What a crazy party. Were there even any other guests there? Lou was conscious that another couple had entered the room, but they seemed a little blown away at what they found. Lou could tell the male of the couple was keen to get stuck in with them, but the female was looking partly horrified and was making sure she reined him in. Lou felt sorry for him. He would have had a ball!

All change please and Lou, despite the action she was having, was getting rather peeved with Pants. He was now giving oral to Rebecca, and Lou wondered what the hell had happened to their pre-party arrangement? He was like a dog on heat; only he didn't seem to want her. And Lou didn't take too kindly to that. Maybe it was because he knew they would be in the hotel later, so he didn't have to impress her. She was a 'given'. Either way, Lou was a little put out to say the least.

In all the fun and swapping, Lou made sure she was safe (sexually), well as safe as you can be while having many partners in close proximity. While condoms protect you from diseases and babies, there's always the risk of transmitting something orally, and giving blow jobs with a rubber layer between you and flesh isn't ideal, although Lou had

VANILLA EXTRACT

done this before. So when Pants exited Lucy, condom still adorned and came at Lou with it at the ready, she got really annoyed. "Are you having a fucking laugh?" As if he expected to enter Lou with a used condom on, even if he hadn't cum in it? "Oh no, I was gonna take it off and get a new one." Bloody liar. Lou knew he had no intention of doing that and brushed him away. Cheeky git!

The girls were back now to having a laugh together. Sam was demonstrating his gush-making abilities and made Lucy and Lou gush at the same time while over each other and him. That took some skills! The ladies were impressed. When they then demonstrated to him that they could do it to each other too, there was a round of applause. It was some show, after all. Shame about the drenched bed, sofa and carpet in that room. They would take some drying out!

Pants had disappeared off and wasn't to be seen for a couple of hours. He was steadily making his way around the venue, pleasuring and being pleasured as he went. Lou and the others had straightened themselves up and were now downstairs enjoying some of the buffet food and chatting about the night so far. Lou explained why she was pissed off with Pants. The others hadn't realised that despite coming here with him, that they had not actually played together. Lucy suggested she go back to their hotel with her and Sam after instead and continue the party there. Sam was a very good lover, and it was bound to be a lot of fun. Lou was very tempted, although she would be stranded and all of her things were at Pants' hotel, including her change of clothes, purse and house keys. She was stuck! It was annoying but hey ho, time to have some more laughs now and not let it spoil the evening.

And so to the dance floor. The strategically placed pole saw some interesting action as the rather tipsy ladies attempted some moves in a ploy to look sexy. Some of it was successful, some of it not so, but the girls had a good giggle in their endeavours. They danced until the early hours, and as all women do, they made the most of having female time out together.

'Ta-da! There he is,' Lou thought, as Pants reappeared on the dance floor with the female owner of the house. His sweaty chest was exposed and he ran his fingers through his hair. They'd obviously just come down from one of the bedrooms where they'd been having sex. Making his way across to Lou, he was full of smiles, looking very pleased with himself. "Oh boy, what a night eh Lou?" He was unreal. Lou nodded, "Yeah, great night." He could sense her frosty tone as she carried on dancing with her friends. He looked puzzled. Lou thought he had no idea she was annoyed with him and she was right. "Everything ok?" She motioned for him to join her in the kitchen where she explained exactly why everything was not ok. She also told him she had considered going to Lucy's and he looked genuinely bewildered. "But what about all your stuff?" Sadly that was the reason she

VANILLA EXTRACT

felt she had to accompany him. She had no choice but to go back with him.

This seemed to bring him down to earth. It was the trigger for him to want to leave and as it was nearing 4am, Lou was ready to go too. Rebecca and Chris had left earlier, so Lou said her goodbyes to the others. The cab ride was quiet, and Lou wanted nothing more than to be in her own bed, which obviously couldn't happen, given how much he had drunk.

Lou was freezing and tired. Pants offered to run her a hot bath when they got in, and she graciously accepted. He jumped in the shorter backed edge and gave Lou the head end. It was bliss - well it would have been if she'd had it to herself. Oddly, Lou had the lyrics to a song running through her head, over and over: all about being stuck and wanting to get away. It was a reflection of the situation she found herself in. Actually, and making it worse, she realised she had caused this situation. It was nothing to do with being found in it. She orchestrated the events tonight that led her to being in a hotel room, far from home, with no way of getting back and being totally reliant on someone she hardly knew. What a fool she was.

Pants got out of the bath and asked if she was going to do the same. Lou didn't really want to, to be fair, and she topped up the hot water. She knew he'd be expecting to have her and that was the last thing she wanted right now, and particularly not with him. In no end of his surprises for her tonight, Pants brushed his teeth in the sink next to her and decided to rinse his toothbrush in the bath water she was lying in. For fuck's sake - was he for real? It was apparently his attempt to get her out of the bath and into his bed, he later revealed. Lou just read it as him having absolutely zero respect for her.

Lou got out, dried and got into bed. She was naked, as she always slept, albeit it about a metre away from him. Pants came over to cuddle her, and she could feel his erection in her back. "Look, it's not going to happen," she said. Pants already knew that and had accepted his fate, although it didn't stop him trying now and again in the morning when he met with the same disappointment. There was no way Lou was going to let him near her, not after the combination of shocking behaviours she'd experienced with him. No way!

The car ride home was difficult, with awkward small talk from time to time. Pants asked if he could come in for a coffee when they arrived at hers and she agreed, only because he had driven her home and paid for the hotel. Even then, despite all that had gone on before, he still made advances on her. "Sorry hon', but the timing or the circumstances just didn't work out. No hard feelings," she said. He was disappointed. Ultimately Lou knew he was a good man, just a little jaded by the opportunistic tendencies that completely consumed him. "Well, I was saving the best till last Lou." Yeah right, she thought. 'You're gonna have to do way better than that.'

What followed from this encounter was some time of reflection. Lou realised to some men out there that she, and many other women, were just a 'hole' for them to use. Equally, of course, it was mutual benefiting. She got what she needed and wanted from men, in the same way they did from her. But where had all the respect gone, for others and for herself too? How cheap had she made herself? Was she just an unpaid whore at the beck and call of other party-goers, in the same way they were to her too? Was this really how she wanted to live?

There were many questions going around her head following that evening. Would a vanilla relationship really be all that bad? It was a flavour that sounded appealing right now. To have someone watch your back, be there to support you, share adventures together, even to snuggle up and watch the TV? It didn't sound boring at all. It sounded like bliss after all the craziness Lou had encountered of late. In fact, she realised she'd quite missed it. This partying lark was fun and exciting in its own right, but equally could be mundane and repetitive, as she was starting to accept.

Lou decided to extract herself now from the swinging scene – just how long for she had not decided yet. What she was sure of was that she couldn't continue like this. She was on the road to self-destruction. She needed to have a good look at

VANILLA EXTRACT

her life and seek some normality, whatever that meant.

Lou was not considering abstaining from sex. She knew this would be unrealistic and she enjoyed it too much to give it up. But a time for contemplation was definitely in order - to work out exactly where this journey would lead her next...

...To be continued

VANILLA EXTRACT

Louisa Berry lives in Hertfordshire with her four children. While not on 'Mum-duties,' she works full time in Finance in Canary Wharf, London.

VANILLA EXTRACT

VANILLA EXTRACT